mYS

McIner
The pr

D0099223

/

11-06

OCT   2006

THE PRUDENCE
❦ OF ❦
THE FLESH

Also by Ralph McInerny

Mysteries Set at the University of Notre Dame

On This Rockne   *Emerald Aisle*
Lack of the Irish   *Celt and Pepper*
Irish Tenure   *Irish Coffee*
Book of Kills   *Green Thumb*
                     Irish Gilt

Father Dowling Mystery Series

Her Death of Cold   *Four on the Floor*
The Seventh Station   *Judas Priest*
Bishop as Pawn   *Desert Sinner*
Lying Three   *Seed of Doubt*
Second Vespers   *A Cardinal Offense*
Thicker Than Water   *The Tears of Things*
A Loss of Patients   *Grave Undertakings*
The Grass Widow   *Triple Pursuit*
Getting a Way with Murder   *Prodigal Father*
Rest in Pieces   *Last Things*
The Basket Case   *Requiem for a Realtor*
Abracadaver   *Blood Ties*

Andrew Broom Mystery Series

Cause and Effect   *Mom and Dead*
Body and Soul   *Law and Ardor*
Savings and Loam   *Heirs and Parents*

THE PRUDENCE

❦ OF ❦

THE FLESH

A Father Dowling Mystery

Ralph McInerny

St. Martin's Minotaur
New York

This is a work of fiction. All of the characters, organizations, and events portrayed in this novel are either products of the author's imagination or are used fictitiously.

THE PRUDENCE OF THE FLESH. Copyright © 2006 by Ralph McInerny. All rights reserved. Printed in the United States of America. No part of this book may be used or reproduced in any manner whatsoever without written permission except in the case of brief quotations embodied in critical articles or reviews. For information, address St. Martin's Press, 175 Fifth Avenue, New York, N.Y. 10010.

www.minotaurbooks.com

Library of Congress Cataloging-in-Publication Data

McInerny, Ralph M.
    The prudence of the flesh / Ralph McInerny.—1st ed.
      p. cm.
    "A Father Dowling mystery."
    ISBN-13: 978-0-312-35144-1
    ISBN-10: 0-312-35144-5
    1. Dowling, Father (Fictitious character)—Fiction. 2. Clergy—Fiction. 3. Catholics—Fiction. 4. Illinois—Fiction. 5. Ex-clergy—Fiction. 6. Child sexual abuse by clergy—Fiction. 7. Paternity—Fiction. I. Title.

PS3563.A31166P78 2006
813'.54—dc22

2006040189

First Edition: August 2006

10 9 8 7 6 5 4 3 2 1

For Mike Loux

προτιμᾶν τὴν ἀλήθειαν

1096a16-17

R0021982851

Part One

The Gregory Barrett show on National Public Radio was called *End Notes*, and Marie Murkin, whatever she thought of the usual offerings on this tax-funded liberal network, was an unabashed fan of Gregory Barrett's weekly book reviews and vignettes on the authors he loved.

"Chesterton's Father Brown," Marie sighed. "Whoever thought that NPR would feature such a Catholic author?"

"You like Chesterton?"

"I do. And I say that without having read anything of his, but Gregory Barrett has convinced me that I must."

"I have one or two titles of his."

"Barrett?"

"Chesterton. Of course, reading Father Brown stories would be like a busman's holiday to you, Marie."

"Are they really as good as he says?"

"Yes." Just yes. Chesterton's clerical sleuth had effectively commandeered the genre. Father Dowling doubted that anyone other than Andrew Greeley would dare open himself to comparison with G. K. Chesterton.

"He has to be a Catholic."

"Chesterton was a convert."

Marie gave him a look. "I meant Barrett."

It seemed the path of wisdom not to tell Marie about Gregory Barrett. If she learned that he was a laicized priest, her estimate of *End Notes* would be grievously affected. Still, it was interesting that while Greg might have left the priesthood, he apparently remained in the fold, if *End Notes* was any indication. Roger Dowling had not seen his old classmate in years. Father Dowling passed on the *Father Brown Omnibus* to Marie.

"I read that straight through during a stay in the infirmary at Mundelein."

"They're all here?"

Marie balanced the green-bound volume as if it could scarcely carry the weight of Gregory Barrett's recommendation.

Within two weeks of this conversation, an awed Marie Murkin looked into the pastor's study.

"He called. He's coming to see you."

These remarks were without preamble, and Roger Dowling had no idea who the bearer of the personal pronoun might be.

"Gregory Barrett." Marie whispered the name as if speaking it aloud would profane it.

"When?"

Marie shook her wrist, bringing her watch into visibility. "This afternoon. Of course I told him you were free."

"I gather he is, too?"

A wet and scolding noise issued from the thin lips of the

housekeeper of St. Hilary's. "He asked if Wednesday was your golf day."

"I won't ask what you answered."

"I told him that even if it were, you would be delighted to see him."

"That's true. Did you leave the impression that I golf weekly?"

"It can't hurt you," Marie said enigmatically, and drifted back to her kitchen.

Even if she was out of sight, she was on the qui vive for the sound of the doorbell at three o'clock. Father Dowling heard her scampering down the hall to the front door before the first ring had subsided.

The rate at which people age is irregular, the metabolism of some enabling them to wear decades as if they were but a single day. Gregory Barrett was one of them. The man Marie ushered into Father Dowling's study was all but unchanged from their seminary days. Oh, a gray hair or two, a bit of a paunch when he relaxed, but for all that Gregory Barrett had aged gracefully and all but invisibly.

"You have a great fan in Marie Murkin," Father Dowling told his old classmate. Marie had remained in the doorway, looking at their visitor as if he were a celebrity, which in a way he was.

"I haven't missed a program since I first happened on it."

"When was that, a week ago?"

Marie's reaction was not quite a girlish giggle. "You sound like you know who."

"Marie was especially impressed by your program on Chesterton's Father Brown stories."

Greg took both of Marie's hands in his. "Thank God. I was fearful it was the program I devoted to Philip Roth."

"You are doing a great work," Marie said, and then actually choked up and ran off to her kitchen.

"She means it," Roger Dowling said. "Marie is incapable of dissembling, and as for flattery, well, she never indulges."

"Oh, I don't know. She was telling me how much you have done for St. Hilary's."

"Even Homer nods."

"*Etiam Homerus dormitat.*" Barrett beamed. "Have you noticed how many such allusions go right over people's heads now?"

"You have."

"Roger, the new illiteracy is beyond belief. Do you know Thomas De Koninck's *La nouvelle ignorance*?"

"I feel I am being given an assignment."

"You'd love it."

"What an interesting career you have devised."

"*End Notes*? I would starve if that were all I did. I have a faculty appointment at Loyola since returning to the area."

"The Jesuits?"

"There aren't that many around." Thus the great topic was introduced. "This house brings it all back. What a nice parish plant you have, Roger."

"It was considered exile when I was assigned here."

"At Mundelein it would have seemed a dream appointment."

Mundelein, all those years ago, and Quigley Prep before that. How their paths had diverged.

"You teach literature?"

"Would that I did. No, I am in something called religious

studies. Meaning an occasion for skeptics and unbelievers to trash the credulity of the simple."

"Tell me about it."

Gregory sat back in his chair and studied Father Dowling. "I have often wondered what someone like you made of those of us who went over the wall."

"My own career has been a bit checkered."

"Roger, here you are, all these years later. That kind of stability should be celebrated. I have come to think that people who keep their lifetime promises are heroes and heroines, if there are any."

"There are no heroes at St. Hilary's. Except maybe Marie Murkin."

"For liking *End Notes*?"

"It is a good program, Greg."

"Have you heard it?"

"Many times. I missed the one on Chesterton but marveled at you on Paul Claudel. Could any of your listeners actually read him?"

"The NPR audience is pretty sophisticated, Roger."

"You mean they would understand about Homer nodding?"

Roger had been filling his pipe and now put a match to it. Greg watched this ritual with awed satisfaction. "You still smoke!"

"You make it sound temporary."

"Roger, it is the only commandment remaining. The decalogue has become a monologue. Thou shalt not smoke. Don't look too carefully at all the dreadful things we actually are doing and concentrate on the high immorality of smoking. Of course, morality has become largely a matter of issuing prohibitions to others on activities that do not tempt us."

"I sometimes think that is one of my motives for continuing. Pipes are an awful nuisance, you know."

"I remember. I have half a mind to go back to it."

"How did you happen to get interested in Paul Claudel?"

"Need you ask? Old Father Casey at Quigley. Remember when we put on that Marian play of Claudel's?"

"L'annonce faite à Marie."

"Exactly. Do you know, I have come to believe that we acquire all our real influences before we are twenty."

Roger pointed to a shelf. "There are Claudel's journals, the Bibliothèque de la Pléiade edition." The volumes had the used look of a set of breviaries, and no wonder. For years, they had been Father Dowling's bedtime reading.

"I have them."

"Why am I not surprised?"

"Casey got flakier and flakier. What was his nickname?" Barrett asked.

"Equivocal. Equivocal Casey." The name brought forth a smile from both men.

"At the end, he was advocating the ordination of women."

"He told you that?"

"Roger, he was the only old prof I felt I could go back and talk to."

In the ensuing silence, Roger Dowling thought how lonely the life of an ex-priest must be. Those who had left the seminary before ordination were consigned to a kind of limbo, off the radar screen, and as for priests who applied for laicization, well . . . The camaraderie of the priesthood was reserved for those who stayed the course. The fact that this was his first meeting with no-longer-Father Gregory Barrett suggested to

Roger Dowling that his old classmate had been hesitant to look him up.

"Did you share his flakier sentiments?"

Greg's eyes roamed along the shelves of the book-lined study. "I sometimes think that my mind-set is ferociously pre–Vatican II. I suppose that surprises you."

"Would you want it to?"

"I can't tell you how good it is to see you after all these years."

"Amen. What prompted you to call?"

A bout of nostalgia threatened, and Roger Dowling wanted to head it off. There had been a lot of changes in the Church since the close of Vatican II in 1965, and about them there were two schools of thought. Some thought all change an improvement; others saw any change as a loss. Accordingly, the past was regarded either as a lost golden age or as a dark period when incredible nonsense reigned. Roger Dowling was in neither camp: Some changes had been good, others bad, so, like the past, they made up a mixed bag.

"I am going to be sued, Roger. Not just me, the archdiocese."

"Good Lord."

"A woman has recently been led to remember that I abused her years ago, before I left. That's what brings the chancery into it. One of their lawyers asked to see me. Do you know Amos Cadbury?"

"I do. As far as I know, the archdiocese is not his client."

"They asked him to do this as a special mission."

"And you saw him."

Gregory nodded. "It was like going to confession to a patriarch."

Roger Dowling smiled. "Amos is a good and just man."

"I wish I could say that my denial I ever knew the woman convinced him."

"Well, he is a lawyer."

"It was when I mentioned that we were classmates that he asked me to come see you. He said he would want to consult you in canon law, so he asked that I tell you everything. I can only tell you what I told him. The name of the woman means nothing to me. Madeline Murphy. Her photograph is of a stranger. Of course, all this was supposed to have happened years ago, when I was an assistant at St. Bavo's."

"Is there anything of that kind to remember?"

"Roger, I was a total celibate until I left." He smiled wryly. "And for some time afterward. No, there was nothing. Oh, maybe a sin of thought, but never anything more."

"No special friendships?" Father Dowling was applying yet another match to his pipe.

Greg opened his hands. Roger would not have been surprised to hear his visitor intone *Orate fratres*. "I have been married for nearly twenty years. Nancy and I have a son, a teenager now. If I had stayed in Cairo this might not have happened."

The pronunciation told Roger Dowling that it was the city in southern Illinois rather than in Egypt that was meant. Greg had taught in a prep school there. Several guest appearances on NPR had led to other things, and finally to the book show that had brought him back to Chicago, where condensed versions of his program appeared as a column in the Sunday *Tribune*.

"And now you're teaching at Loyola."

"I had an offer from Knox as well, but we wanted to live close to Chicago."

"Knox."

"It sounds like those old jokes, doesn't it? Knock knock."

"Who's there?"

"Me, almost. Maybe if I had gone there this wouldn't have happened. God only knows what publicity of this kind will do to me. But that isn't the worst of it."

"Your family."

"Of course. The first call came to Nancy. My wife. But you and all the others, Roger. To think I should be an instrument of such treatment of the priesthood."

"Some of it seems deserved."

"Not this time, Roger. Not this time. The archdiocese's lawyers suggested that some kind of settlement be made, to keep it out of the media."

"Amos suggested that?"

"He vetoed it. He also vetoed my suggestion that I countersue. He seems to have as glum an impression of the law as the media have of the priesthood."

It was clear that this would not be a solo visit. Once Roger Dowling spoke with Amos Cadbury, the charges against Gregory Barrett would be a continuous concern of the pastor of St. Hilary's. Did he believe Barrett? He found that he did. Of course, memories of innocence can be as unreliable as those of guilt.

"What a lovely man." Marie sighed. Barrett had dallied at the doorway with her before going out to his car.

"He's already married."

"If I wanted to marry every man I admired, I would have to move out of the rectory."

On that enigmatic note she left him, and Father Dowling stared after her as if he had just moved some small fraction of the way into the equivocal position in which a woman's accusation had put Gregory Barrett. Of course, Marie was of an age, and whatever bloom she had known in youth had long since faded away—but we live in odd times when public sensuality of a kind that would have shamed the pagan Romans goes hand in hand with puritanical moralizing.

He went back to his study and had another pipe.

Amos Cadbury had spent a long lifetime in the practice of law and had become a student of his profession's history. Anton Chroust's two-volume account of the legal profession in the United States had for him the added attraction of having been written by one of his old professors, but it was to Cicero that Amos went for some rough parallel to his own situation. As the republic dissolved and gave way to Caesar, Cicero had to plead for justice in a society where justice was only a word, and that largely the word of one man. Of course, it was the oldest challenge of all: how to do well in circumstances that often leave everything to be desired.

Such thoughts had enabled Amos to continue into advanced old age until he was now one of the venerables of the Chicago area bar, many of whose members he could no longer admire. The parlous condition of the legal profession was one thing—a comparatively minor thing, Amos would think in the privacy of his own mind—but what was happening to the Catholic priesthood in the media was a grave matter indeed. In his lifetime, Amos had known many priests. Many he had liked, and others he could only venerate for their office, but never to his knowledge had he known a libertine priest of the kind that was now almost daily thrust upon the public. It was so painful a subject he had never even discussed it with Roger Dowling, although the pastor of St. Hilary's was Amos's favorite counterexample of the tragic clerics now being paraded before the prurient public eye.

Amos had never dreamt he would be professionally involved in this tragedy, but when Robert Barfield asked him in the bar of the University Club if he would help the chancery in this case, he could scarcely refuse.

"My first thought was to include his in a cluster of cases we are negotiating." Barfield spoke into his brandy as if a microphone might be hidden in the balloon glass.

"Negotiating."

"It is surprising how money soothes the victims. But Madeline Murphy was not interested in money."

No wonder Barfield was known as Bartering Bob. His idea of law was to avoid court as much as possible, and a jury like the plague. In the case of abusive priests, this might have seemed the counsel of prudence.

"What did Barrett think of negotiating?"

"He refused. He didn't even hesitate. Maybe he is innocent."

"Maybe."

"Doesn't the accused always protest his innocence?"

"Would you?"

Barfield allowed a slow smile to form on his wide mouth. "That's a logical trap, isn't it?"

"A variation on the Liar's Paradox?"

Barfield sent him what he had on Gregory Barrett, and then Amos met the accused. In the meantime, he had listened to a number of his radio programs and had been surprised by the tone of his oral essays on authors and books he loved. The program was unashamedly personal. If Barrett always offered the basis for his likings, he never elevated this estimate into an absolute standard. *"De gustibus,"* he once began, and then quickly corrected himself, putting the thought into English. On another occasion, when he might have said *corruptio optimi pessima*, he offered a beautiful poetic equivalent: *Lilies that fester smell worse than weeds.* Before he met him, Amos wondered if Gregory Barrett had found the appropriate motto for himself and other shepherds who had turned into wolves.

"How long were you a priest?" Amos had begun, all business.

"Oh, one is always that, you know."

"You believe that?"

"It's not a personal opinion."

"And yet you left."

"You must remember what it was like, after the council. It was hard not to be influenced by all that commotion. Nuns were leaving, classmate after classmate left, it became a flood. I began to wonder if I would be the last one left and have to turn out the lights."

Amos thought about that. It was difficult not to see the parallel with his own misgivings about the legal profession. The thought of retiring to his cabin on the shores of a Wisconsin lake was powerfully attractive. Cicero would have been well advised to do what Horace did: get out of town, away from the wicked city. Horace managed to die a natural death. Barrett made his leaving sound like something less than desertion.

"Now, this woman, Madeline Murphy. You don't remember her?"

"I am certain I never so much as knew her."

"She was a parishioner at St. Bavo's when you were an assistant pastor there."

"I must have been shown a recent photograph."

"How so?"

"I thought she must have been a child all those years ago."

"She was sixteen."

"Sixteen!" Barrett sat back.

The woman had said it all began when she went to confession to then-Father Barrett. That would have added sacrilege to mere moral turpitude. Many of the current accusations against the clergy made Boccaccio seem deficient in imagination.

"And I am guilty until proved innocent?"

"It is difficult to prove a negative."

"Then all it takes is an accusation. The chancery lawyer actually advised me to come to terms."

"I know. Apparently the woman was unwilling."

"I would have thought that was all she wanted, money."

"I understand Barfield's suggestion. Keeping such things out of the media is a way of protecting the Church."

"And of encouraging blackmail."

"It isn't always blackmail."

"Well, it is this time. You say my innocence can't be proved. At least it can be asserted. Even if she were paid off, there is no guarantee of future silence."

"She would have to agree to that in any settlement."

"And what penalty if she later broke that agreement?"

Amos found Barrett difficult to understand, but, of course, there was the enormous obstacle of realizing that the expensively dressed and distinguished middle-aged man was in fact a priest, a status that could not be removed by laicization. *Thou art a priest forever.* That made Barrett as much a priest as Father Dowling. It turned out that they had been classmates.

"So you know Roger," Barrett said.

"I thought of him because he is a canon lawyer."

"You don't imagine that this accusation will be tried by the Church?"

Once, of course, that would have been the proper venue of such a charge, but the churches had long since appealed to the civil courts to adjudicate internal matters, and that had made the civic arm less reluctant to look the other way when clerical misbehavior became known. He told Barrett that he would consult with Father Dowling and then they would meet again.

"Maybe I'll go see Roger myself."

"I was about to suggest that."

So it was that Amos Cadbury got involved in a scandal that had caused him and the laity so much anguish. The bishops seemed to have but two recourses in dealing with accusations against priests: to the civil law and to psychological counseling. It was the latter that had prompted them to cover up for erring clerics for so long, sending them off to clinics to be talked to and redefined in therapeutic terms. That many of the offenders returned to active duty and their old practices did not seem to dim the confidence of many prelates that a wayward priest was simply a mind in need of a few adjustments through counseling. No wonder the whole sad business had finally ended in the criminal courts. Now the bishops spoke of civic prosecution as if it were an arm of their own governance. The one word that was never mentioned was "sin." Nor did the bishops seem to realize their own responsibility for what had happened. However small a percentage of the priestly population these sexual predators were, one of them was too many, yet some of the most egregious seemed enabled by the treatment they had received from their spiritual superiors. The bishops' response was now something called zero tolerance. This policy effectively put all priests under suspicion and elevated bishops high above the fray. Yet there had also been a few bishops whose pasts turned out to be vulnerable to accusation—a few, but was the percentage of bishops lower than that of the priests? No wonder it was tempting to imagine a flying squad of Swiss Guards swooping down and carrying all the offenders off to the Castel San Angelo, where oubliettes awaited them.

Those who saw Ned Bunting prominent in the aisles of St. Bavo's Church on Sunday at the ten o'clock Mass, imperiously signaling latecomers into the front pews, taking up the collection with something of the insistence of the IRS, would scarcely have realized that this restless usher was an aspiring author. It was, of course, a well-kept secret. The only person Ned had ever confided in was fellow parishioner Gloria Daley.

"What have you written?"

"I doubt you would have read it."

"That dirty?"

He winked and looked away. Being thought of as a racy author was better than not being thought of as an author at all. Should he show Gloria some of his stuff? He frowned away the thought. It wasn't only that she might expect steamy fare and be disappointed. Ned's experience of letting others read his things was not encouraging.

Fifteen years ago, when he had decided that he would stop just thinking about it and get to work writing, he had sent a manuscript off for evaluation. For a fee, of course. The first evaluation simply paraphrased what he had written and advised him to read Faulkner, and that was that. No suggestion at all that they would try to market the story, although that promise had seemed implicit in the advertisement that had induced Ned to enclose a fifty-dollar check with his manuscript. The evaluation ended with the suggestion that a deeper and more technical evaluation could perhaps be helpful. Ned took the bait. Before he was done, he had spent five hundred dollars and his manuscript was no nearer to being published. He had rewritten the story four times, following different and conflicting advice. Now when he looked back at his original version, he was sure it was better than any of the revisions. He swore never to be taken in again.

During the long disappointing years, he had kept his promise. He only broke it last spring when the notice of a writers' meeting announced that evaluations of one's work by editors and agents attending would be available. Ned looked over his collected works—he now had thirty-one completed stories in his files— picked what he considered the best, which was also the most recent, and sent it to the conference organizers with his check.

At the meeting, he was scheduled for an hour with Max Zubiri, an editor who had been on the staffs of a dozen magazines and was now a book editor in a famous old house. For a half minute after Ned sat across from him, Zubiri stared at him silently.

"This your first story?" he finally said.

"First! There are dozens more where that came from."

"I was afraid of that."

"What do you mean?"

"If this was your first try, it would be easier for you to face the fact that you will never be a writer."

Ned was more stunned than angry. "You call this an evaluation!"

"Oh, we'll go over what you've written."

Maybe the Last Judgment will be like that, but Ned was sure it would be easier than the clinical way in which Zubiri pointed out the deficiencies in what he had written. The pages of the manuscript were covered with the editor's comments.

"But that's just technical stuff. Maybe someday you could learn what the hell a story is. It won't matter. Is English your native tongue?"

Ned managed to get to his feet, but no appropriately crushing response came to mind. His brain seemed to be on fire, all his hopes going up in the flames of his anger. He turned and got to the door of the room.

"Take this with you," Zubiri called after him. He was waving the curled and commented-on pages of Ned's story. Then a response came, arising out of the basement of Ned Bunting's soul, where bric-a-brac from his army days jostled with crude messages from rest-room walls. He flung it back at Zubiri, whose only reaction was to stuff the manuscript into the wastebasket beside him rather than into his ear.

Ned thought of complaining to the conference organizers. He listened to two authors who had known success in a tenth of the time Ned had devoted to failure. Persistence. Keep at it. Their advice came down to that. Ned could have wept. When the young woman of the pair spoke of her eternal gratitude to Max Zubiri, her editor, Ned left the talk, checked out of the hotel, and drove home to Fox River, a journey of which he retained no memory at all. It was like coming home drunk, only what he was was sober. It took him a week before he convinced himself that Zubiri's word could not be the last. In his search for a way of proving himself, he hit on the idea of writing a brief column for the Sunday parish bulletin.

"Not as long as yours, of course," he told the pastor, Monsignor Sledz. "Maybe a hundred, a hundred and fifty words."

"How long would you say mine is?"

"Five hundred words."

"I never count them."

"It's pretty good."

Monsignor Sledz had one of those Polish baby faces. His cheeks turned a little pink, but Ned did not like the gleam in the monsignor's blue eyes.

"And you want to write a column."

"I could show you some samples."

"A few words from the usher?"

"Oh, I wouldn't refer to what I do in the parish."

"You find seats for people at Mass. You take up the collection." There was an edge to the pastor's voice.

"That's what an usher does, yes."

"You could call it 'The Fall of the House of Usher.'" The monsignorial smile was mean. Ned might have been facing Zubiri again. "Sure, send me a sample. Why don't you ask the other ushers to do the same?"

Ned quit as an usher. He would have liked to submit his resignation, but the truth was, it was a voluntary position. Sometimes they just invited people out of the pews to help take up the collection. Quitting meant not going back to St. Bavo's. Maybe he would quit going to Mass altogether. Who was tormenting him here, Zubiri and Sledz, or God himself? Why had he been plagued by his ambition to be a writer only to open himself to such crushing humiliation? It was during those dark days that he met Gloria.

She was behind him in the checkout line at the supermarket and twice ran her cart against his ankles. The second time, she circled the cart and squeezed his arm when she said she was sorry.

"Think nothing of it."

"You like it? I'll do it again."

And she did, gently, and they both laughed. He waited while she paid for her own things.

"Watch it," she said. "I still have my cart."

He took over from her, offering to push her cart to her car.

"Once an usher, always an usher," she replied. He stopped and stared at her, ready for anything after Zubiri and Sledz, but her smile was not cruel. "Sundays you look so goody-goody. I bet you're a terror on weekdays."

"Word gets around."

At her car, she took bags from the cart and handed them to him so he could put them in the trunk. It doubled the work, but he was sorry when the cart was empty.

"Now show me to my pew."

"Did I ever do that?"

"I'm not that kind of girl."

What was she—fifty, late forties? No, fifty at least. He felt he would have remembered her face if he had noticed her before: pretty, surrounded by ringlets because she pulled her winter cap tight on her head, but it was the lips Ned noticed, and the eyes.

"What kind are you?"

"Give me a ring and find out." She jabbed him in the side with her mittened hand. "I mean a phone call."

"I don't have your number."

"Don't be so sure." She scrawled it on one of the grocery bags and tore it off, sending oranges running around in her trunk. They made teamwork of correcting that, too. "I even know your name. I asked another girl who that good-looking usher at ten o'clock was."

"What's your name?"

"Gloria. Bye-bye."

It was ridiculous. She drove away before Ned realized he had emptied his groceries into her trunk as well. Would he ever have called her if it weren't for that?

Marie Murkin couldn't believe it the first time she saw Ned Bunting at Mass in St. Hilary's. She was so surprised that she didn't confront him and ask when he had stopped going to St. Bavo's. A few months ago, Marie had filled in at St. Bavo's while the housekeeper was on vacation, adding that task to her work at St. Hilary's.

"Can't they cook for themselves for a week? Or eat out?" Father Dowling asked.

"If you don't want me to . . ."

"There are three priests there, you know. Polish parishes haven't been hit as hard."

"Well, they'll have to eat American if I cook for them. I explained that to Barbara."

"They'll try to hire you away from me."

Marie was frowning lest a silly smile break out. It was nice to know she was appreciated. She meant it, too: One more remark and she would call Barbara and tell her Father Dowling had vetoed the idea. She couldn't let her old friend down like that, though. For an anxious moment, she wondered if Father Dowling was teasing her. He was always teasing her.

"Oh, go. I suppose it's far more likely that some man will sweep you off your feet and take you away."

If any man could have, and of course the idea was ridiculous, it was someone like Ned Bunting, the chief usher at St. Bavo's. Not that they had ranks, but anyone seeing Ned at work would know he was in charge. Barbara had mentioned him to Marie before leaving on her Warsaw trip, a gift from the pastor. Of course, Barbara was her age; well, close—in any case, older than Ned Bunting. Imagine Marie's reaction when she herself began to go gaga over Ned. She didn't have to imagine the teasing Father Dowling would give her if he suspected she was smitten by a man, and by such a young man.

The second time he came to Mass at St. Hilary's there was a woman with him.

Marie called Barbara at St. Bavo's and asked her to come for tea on her next afternoon off. They had a wonderful time at the kitchen table. Barbara was full of stories about Monsignor Sledz and did not expect Marie to reply in kind.

"Why are your ushers now coming to Mass here?"

Barbara sat back and puffed out her cheeks. "You mean Ned Bunting. Sledz drove him away. He had them all laughing at Ned Bunting's idea that he write a weekly column for the parish bulletin. I haven't seen him in church since I heard the story."

"He and his wife were here a week ago."

"Wife? He's not married."

"Oh, really."

"Such a fine figure of a man. He's half Polish, you know."

"I wonder who she is."

"When you find out, let me know."

So much for that avenue. Barbara did not seem reluctant to let the subject drop. Two days later, though, she called.

"The woman you saw with Ned Bunting? Her name is Gloria Daley. Our organist knows her."

There was a scary moment when Marie feared that Barbara would say something about her curiosity, but that, too, passed. Marie resolved to drive the thought from her mind. What on earth difference did it make to her where Ned Bunting went to church and with whom? Then she saw the two of them in the supermarket and managed to keep several aisles between them and herself. Even so, she could hear the woman's trilling laughter. Why do some women make such a fuss over a man?

Tuttle of Tuttle & Tuttle did not recognize the name of the man who came to him, but then he had no time to listen to the radio. When does anyone listen to the radio except in his car? As often as not, the car Tuttle was in was driven by Peanuts Pianone, who was on the lowest rung in the Fox River police but nonetheless a valuable source of information for the battling attorney. If Tuttle waited for legal business to come to him, he would have given up long ago. So it was a good day when Hazel informed him that a potential client would be in the office at ten the following morning.

"That's a little early, isn't it?"

"Not for the birds. Be here."

How entrenched Hazel had become since he had first brought her aboard as a temporary. Before her week was out, she had established herself in the outer office. Already you would have thought that he worked for her. Peanuts refused to visit the office now, even when tempted with a promise of a feast of sent-for Chinese food. Now they only enjoyed Chinese food together at the Great Wall restaurant or as now, in Peanuts's unmarked car. Hazel had reached Tuttle through his cell phone and barked instructions about the next morning's appointment.

"That her?" Peanuts asked, delicately holding the chopsticks with which he was transferring sweet and sour chicken to his mouth, meeting it halfway.

Tuttle nodded. There was no way he could fool Peanuts when it came to Hazel, but it had been a long time since he had even permitted himself to wonder what it would be like without Hazel in the office. Her manner did not intimidate clients as it did Tuttle, one of those little mysteries of life. Another was why she stayed with him. She could have browbeaten a whole firm and made a real name for herself.

Peanuts already had the name—"Bitch"—but then Peanuts was overtly the male chauvinist that Tuttle was only *in petto*. Odd that the dumbo Peanuts understood the phrase. Of course, he was Italian. Hazel wasn't even his least favorite. His real grievance was Agnes Lamb, the black cop who had easily soared beyond him. When racism could be added to misogyny, you had Peanuts.

The man gave his name as William Arancia. Tuttle knew from the start he was lying. What else are lawyers for?

"I don't really approve of what I am asking you to do. I want a person looked into."

"Purpose?"

"Can we just call it curiosity?"

"Okay. What's her name?"

"Madeline Murphy."

"Wife? Fiancée? Just friend?"

"None of the above. She may represent a threat to me and my family."

"Ah. Blackmail?"

"You could call it that."

"I could call it anything. What do you call it?"

"Blackmail."

Tuttle took down what particulars William Arancia could give him on Madeline Murphy. Finally he stopped him. "What do you need me for?"

"That's what I hope you will find out."

Tuttle already knew his first job would be to find out the real name of his client. The man had no hesitation in paying Tuttle a hundred dollars to seal their relation as lawyer and client. In cash. Good. Why confuse the IRS with recorded payments?

When Tuttle had shown his new client out, warning him that the elevator was temporarily out of commission, he turned to a beaming Hazel. "Tuttle, that man has class," she said.

"I wonder what his name is."

"I told you his name. Don't you remember anything?"

Standing over Hazel's desk, he called Peanuts and asked what *arancia* meant.

"Orange. But your secretary's a *limone*."

Having hung up, Tuttle asked Hazel, "Would you have believed him if he said he was William of Orange?"

"Is that his real name?"

"You don't know the name of the man all Irishmen hate?"

"Tuttle?"

Never apologize, never explain. Arguments with Hazel were

pointless. Either she won, and was obnoxious for days, or lost, and was worse.

Later, in his own car, Tuttle turned on the radio and heard the unmistakable voice of his new client. He pulled over and listened to a pretty impenetrable talk on Ronald Firbank. "The title of one of his novels poses the same problem nowadays as the title of one of Conrad's. *Prancing Nigger*, like *The Nigger of the 'Narcissus'* . . ." Tuttle was glad Peanuts wasn't with him. Not until the end of the program did the speaker identify himself. "This is Gregory Barrett, with *End Notes*. I'll be back again next week. Meanwhile . . ."

Tuttle turned off the radio, then turned it on again to see what station it was. Gregory Barrett. The name meant nothing to him—but it would. He wasn't going to begin looking into the life of Madeline Murphy until he knew exactly who he was working for. Whom? The program had the odd effect of making Tuttle wonder if he knew the English language.

Gloria Daley agreed with Ned Bunting about Monsignor Sledz, although on a different basis. She said that the pastor at St. Bavo's had laughed away her questions about obtaining an annulment.

"Marriage is permanent, my dear lady. That's the idea, and it should drive out every other idea."

Gloria had tried to appeal to what she read in the papers—annulments were had almost for the asking, in the eyes of critics—but she never even got to ask.

"An annulment," Ned repeated. You only needed an annulment if you were married, and he had not thought of Gloria as married. How had he thought of her? A youngish aunt, full of fun, one who didn't question his claim to be a writer.

"Fortunately, or I should say unfortunately, it all resolved itself."

"How so?"

"He died. In a far-off land." Her eyes drifted away as her voice lowered. Then she turned and smiled, and he knew the theatrics were a put-on. "Iraq."

"Ah."

"You didn't think I'd lead you on if I were a married woman, did you?"

Was she leading him on? Ned had little experience of women, and he doubted that experience would have helped with Gloria. How old was she, anyway? The way she poked him in the ribs when she spoke to him might have been just a joke, like the theatrics, but now she was running her hand along his arm, asking him to tell her what Monsignor Sledz had done to him.

"I told you I'm a writer."

"But you haven't let me see any of your dirty books."

It had been a mistake to let her believe that he wrote off-color stuff. That made it more difficult to speak of the treatment his proposal to write a column for the parish bulletin had received. When he did, Gloria's reaction was a tonic.

"Why should you demean yourself writing for that silly bulletin?"

"It *was* a stupid idea, but I had just finished a story, and the thought came, and I talked to the ineffable Sledz, and here we are."

She had been following what he said with bright eyes, and when he said "ineffable" he felt her hand tighten on his arm. He had learned that unusual words triggered deep emotions in her. Now she lifted her face, eyes half closed, and it was the most natural thing in the world to kiss her. He put his lips to hers briefly, then withdrew.

"The kiss of peace," she murmured.

"Don't be sacrilegious."

"I meant that you could get away with that in church." She lifted her face again. The second kiss would have been inappropriate in church, except perhaps at the conclusion of a wedding. The thought made him wary. Gloria's talk of an annulment, the lost husband, her undeniable warmth—it all suggested that she was shopping for a replacement.

"I'll never marry again," she sighed, as if reading his fears.

"I never have."

"Wise man. But then you have your writing."

"What I need at the moment is a project, an idea, something big. Henry Drummond?" Drummond, a Former Archdiocesan employee, loudly accused the Cardinal and his minions of injustice.

If she registered this remark, she gave no indication of it. She wanted to talk about priests and the way some of them were making the news lately. Gloria said she found them less intimidating now that all that dirty linen was being aired in public. For all they knew, Monsignor Sledz . . . The thought ended in hysterical laughter. The laughter subsided, and Gloria sat back and looked at Ned with what he thought of as her significant look.

"Why not that?" she asked.

"Why not what?"

"For your new project. A book on this scandal. It just goes on and on. Don't forget that even Cardinal Bernardin had to answer a silly accusation. What do you think?"

There are moments, and this was one of them, when out of booming buzzing confusion an idea emerges that has the mark of destiny on it. Of course. This was his subject. After years at St. Bavo's, he knew a thing or two about the clergy. Nothing scandalous there, certainly, but he thought he understood the clerical mind.

"What there is of it," Gloria said, wrinkling her nose.

"The question is how to approach the subject."

They went to work on it, the two of them. It was the first brainstorming Ned Bunting had ever engaged in.

Suddenly Gloria was on her feet. She walked back and forth in her living room, striking her forehead and groaning. "My God, I've got it." She rejoined him on the couch, taking his hands in hers. "I have a friend . . ." She stopped and inhaled. "A friend who is a victim. Isn't that where to begin, with the victims?"

Thus it was that Ned Bunting first heard of Madeline Murphy. Later he came to think that Gloria's sudden inspiration for his new writing project was not as spontaneous as it appeared, owing much to her theatrical ability for seeming so.

7

"What bothers me," Amos Cadbury said to Roger Dowling, "is the way these scandals affect priests like yourself."

"Little if at all, Amos."

"But surely the way the priesthood is made fun of nowadays is something new."

"Maybe overdue, in a way. Oh, these scandals pain me, Amos, but there is also the realization that there but for the grace of God go I. As for being made fun of, there are a lot worse things."

"I am beginning to think that Gregory Barrett should have tried to conceal his case in the bundle of them Barfield is negotiating."

"Oh?"

"The woman has been trying to see Barrett's wife."

In this Barrett was unlike the other objects of such accusations: He had left the priesthood, married, and established a career. Perhaps as a former priest he thought he was less vulnerable, but having a family was its own kind of vulnerability. The celibate can suffer alone, whether deservedly or not, but

Gregory Barrett had a wife and son and could not ignore the effect on them of the charge brought against him.

"It may sound cynical to say so, Father, but I think the media prefer to bay after a man who still wears a Roman collar and is involved in priestly work. Someone like Barrett requires too much explanation."

They were in Amos's office awaiting the arrival of Gregory Barrett to discuss the charges against him. When he was announced and came into the office, Roger Dowling thought his classmate looked a good deal less self-possessed than he had a week before at the St. Hilary rectory. He almost collapsed into the chair Amos pointed him to.

"She telephoned again last night. Mr. Cadbury, I think I should bring a suit against her."

"I hope it never comes to that. Actually, these telephone calls may prove helpful."

"You wouldn't say that if you knew what they're doing to us. Can you imagine what it's like for me to discuss such an accusation with my wife? Of course she believes me, but what a subject to test her trust on. It's our son she's afraid for."

Roger said, "Does he know your past?"

"That is the problem. We decided long ago that we would make a complete break. The past would be as if it had never been. That worked in Cairo. It was coming back to the Chicago area that brought this on."

"In what way?"

"That woman must have listened to my program."

"Does she have a lawyer?" Amos asked.

"I haven't any idea."

"If she calls again, urge her to acquire a lawyer, someone I can discuss this with."

A cadre of lawyers dedicated to exposing clerical scandals moved across the country from diocese to diocese, coordinating their efforts and bringing media pressure on bishops as well as on the accused. Huge sums of money had been paid out, and there seemed no end to the cases that were turned up. One or two had been truly shocking, exhibiting a pattern of perversity extending over many years. It was a tragic thing to see a man in his eighties confronting accusations from decades ago, but in most cases indictment and punishment were long overdue.

What Roger could not fathom was how a man involved in such behavior could go on functioning as a priest. How could such a one give homilies, hear confessions, say Mass? The thought of a man in a state of mortal sin saying Mass brought back that terrible image from the autobiography of St. Teresa of Avila, a vision she had of devils swarming around the altar when Mass was being said by a sinful priest. Not that the acts of the priesthood depended on the personal virtue of the priest. *Ex opere operato*, in the phrase; the priest acted in the name of the Church, not in his own. It was actually a heresy to hold that only a good priest could do the deeds of the priest. For all that, the function called for more than ordinary virtue, for an exemplary life. The faithful had a right to expect priests to be better than themselves, or at least to be trying to be better. *We are symbols of more than ourselves*, he thought. *That is why our misdeeds have such a devastating impact.*

No need to dwell on the prurience of the media in reporting the stories. No need to point out that other professions were not targets of the effort to discredit and extort huge compensatory payments. The priesthood was a target unlike any other. That members of it had behaved like libertines was in its way a unique story. Still, Gregory Barrett's case was atypical, and Amos seemed to think it could be handled in a delicate way.

In the elevator, going down, Greg said, "I wonder if he is the type of lawyer one needs in a situation like that."

"Amos is the best."

"Has he ever been in a gutter fight? Wouldn't it make sense to find out what we can about this girl?"

"The accuser?"

"Yes. What kind of person claims to remember such things long afterward? Do they just pop into the mind? I don't understand all this suppressed memory stuff. It sounds to me like the result of suggestion."

"Memory is an odd faculty."

"When it comes down to it, I think we are going to have to fight fire with fire. Or mud with mud."

They had arranged to meet Greg's wife for a drink at the Palmer House.

It was difficult to think that Nancy Barrett had ever been a nun. Her hair was silver gray, but her face was as youthful as Greg's. She put out her hand when her husband introduced Father Dowling, and as he took it he looked into her cool blue eyes. In the bar, the Barretts ordered martinis and Father Dowling mineral water. Almost immediately they were discussing the great topic.

"I never before wanted to kill someone," Nancy Barrett said. She paused. "I suppose I can want to now only because she is a stranger."

William Arancia had turned out to be Gregory Barrett, adjunct member of the faculty at Loyola and a regular on NPR radio.

"Married, one son, one wife, and a home on a wooded lot."

Tuttle asked Hazel how she had found all this out. She tossed a brochure to him almost disdainfully. It was a promotional piece from NPR, and pictured there among other regulars was Tuttle's client.

"Maybe I should have you find the woman he's interested in."

"You haven't told me anything. So I was lucky to look through that brochure before throwing it out, but how can I be lucky if you don't tell me what or who we're after?"

Did she aspire to be one of the Tuttles in Tuttle & Tuttle? Hazel was what is sometimes called a lot of woman, having in abundance those traits that set the female of the species off from the male. Not a beauty by any means, she was a woman who had known disappointments in the romance department ("Don't ask") but had yet to throw in her cards and accept existence as a single. Tuttle had not often been the object of unmistakable advances from a female, but Hazel when the mood was on her could be blushingly direct. Only a lifetime of terror of such intimacy had enabled Tuttle to escape being taken into her arms and crushed against her enormous bosom. Still, the danger was always there—a danger magnified by the fact that he began to be curious about what it would be like to surrender. He had already surrendered his office to the woman, allowing her to nag him into a subsidiary position. Could he long resist Hazel the next time the fleshly desires were on her?

Now the softness had gone out of Tuttle's attitude toward her, though. She had made a fool of him, finding out all about his client by the simple expedient of reading her junk mail.

"It's a professional secret," he said, and it sounded like a whimper.

Then she realized what she had done, and moved toward him with her chiseled face distorted by compassion. She had him by both wrists before he could escape. She pulled him closer, providing empirical verification that the female body is considerably different from the male.

"Did I hurt your feelings, Isaac?"

That did it. He wrested his wrists free, plucked his Irish tweed hat from its perch, and was out the door in a trice. Nobody called him Isaac and got away with it. He wasn't ashamed of the name, not at all, but he wanted to keep it sacred, a secret between him and his deceased parents, particularly his father. He had been kidded about it at school. In law school he used his initials, I. M., but since opening his office he had been simply Tuttle. Tuttle & Tuttle, the second for his father. Or was it the first? No need to distinguish between Abraham and Isaac Tuttle.

From his car, he called Peanuts, and they met at a new all-you-can-eat self-serve Chinese place. There was a flat fee, and one could load up one's plate as many times as one liked. Peanuts told this to Tuttle as they walked from their cars to the brightly painted storefront. The place was not crowded.

"We're early," Peanuts explained.

"For what? It's going on noon."

Peanuts ignored him. Maybe part of the attraction of the place was the fact that there were not a lot of people Peanuts had to elbow out of the way as he moved along the hot table, taking something of everything. Tuttle took some shrimp fried rice and a bowl of wonton soup.

Peanuts went back to the table three times before he acknowledged Tuttle's companionship. "What's wrong?" he asked.

"Nothing's wrong."

"Something's wrong."

"Peanuts, if something was wrong I'd tell you."

"It's her, isn't it?"

"Yes."

"Get rid of her."

Did Peanuts have any idea of the human wear and tear firing someone exacted? Of course not. It was wrong to feed Peanuts's animosity against Hazel.

"You want me to take care of it?"

Good grief, what did Peanuts think they were talking about? Too late he remembered that, improbable as it was, Peanuts was a member of the locally famous Pianone family, for whom getting rid of someone might mean a one-way trip to the Fox River.

"No! She's really not that bad."

"You act like it."

"Just a bad day."

"Sure. Want some more?"

And back for more food went Peanuts. In a way, what he had offered was a friendly gesture. To Tuttle, not to Hazel. Not for the first time, it occurred to Tuttle that Peanuts might be his best friend, and vice versa. Usually he thought Peanuts got the better of that deal, but not today.

"Peanuts, I meant that about Hazel."

"Okay."

"I mean I don't want to get rid of her."

"You don't have to do nothing."

He ended by pleading for Hazel's life, unsure how serious Peanuts was but not daring to find out. "You can do me a favor, though."

"Name it."

"I'll tell you on the way downtown."

It was a long shot, but Tuttle wondered if there might be information on his client at police headquarters. Now that he knew who Gregory Barrett was, he was more than ever surprised at his coming to Tuttle for help. A man like that went to a lawyer like that, not to Tuttle. This suggested a concern of a kind that Barrett would not like to share with a more respectable attorney.

They commandeered an office with a computer and began to check the database. Peanuts could barely read, but he was a whiz with the computer. His fat little fingers flew over the keyboard, and on the screen data were displayed.

"Zilch."

"It was just a hunch."

"Wait." Peanuts leaned toward the monitor, then tipped it toward Tuttle.

"Gregory Barrett," Tuttle read. "Well, well."

The name occurred in a list of local priests who had been accused of sexual misconduct. Priests? Barrett wasn't a priest—but there his name was, and the name of the woman he had hired Tuttle to find all about: Madeline Murphy. He seemed to have found the reason Gregory Barrett had chosen Tuttle & Tuttle of all the other law firms around.

Gloria Daley had begun painting when she gave up on ever learning how to draw. Color was her strong point anyway. She dabbled a bit in watercolors but was always afraid to use plenty of water. Oils were all right, but acrylics became her medium. Eventually the problem of what to do with all her pictures arose. She gave a lot away; she rented a booth at the Fox River art fair every spring and had actually sold a picture once. Some of them were on display at the Benjamin Harrison branch of the public library, where her friend Madeline worked. Her house was full of them, and it was a big test when she first asked Ned Bunting to her place.

"You're an artist!" he cried.

"Well, I paint a little."

"A little? My God." When he turned to her, his expression was one she hadn't seen before. Then he was gathering her into his arms.

"Does paint do that to you? Maybe I should dab a little behind my ears."

"They're abstract, aren't they?"

"My ears?" She punched him. "How much do you know about art?"

"You are the first artist I've ever met."

"Well, you're my first author. Come, let's get a beer." She had to practically drag him into the kitchen, plunk him in the booth in her kitchenette, and hand him his beer. "I painted this room, too."

He just looked at her, shaking his head back and forth, smiling. She figured at the most he was seven or eight years younger. At St. Bavo's, when he was the usher, she had followed him up and down the aisle with her eyes, trying to figure him out. She liked a tall man, but only if he used his height and didn't stoop, and Ned Bunting went back and forth like a sentinel.

The reason she had asked him over was to meet Madeline. If she had guessed what her paintings would do to Ned, she would have postponed the meeting.

"You have to be gentle with her, Ned. It will just come out. That's how she told me."

Madeline Murphy was a woman of faded prettiness with blondish hair and a doelike wariness in her large brown eyes. She actually tipped her head back to look up at Ned when he held her hand in greeting.

"Ned is the writer I was telling you about, Maddie. He's writing a book about all these priests who, well, you know."

"Oh, yes, I know."

The first time was just a matter of getting acquainted. But

later they got down to business. Ned plugged in his cassette recorder, so he wouldn't have to recharge the batteries. Madeline looked at the machine he had put on the coffee table as if she were afraid of it. She looked away. "Is that new?" She was pointing at an unframed canvas propped against the fireplace tools.

"Do you like it?" Gloria asked.

"Oh, yes."

"Wow, is this my day. You can have it, if you like."

"Oh, I couldn't."

Ned turned off the recorder; no need to waste tape on this. Maybe it wasn't a good idea having Gloria here when he interviewed Madeline.

"All you have to do is talk the way you did before when you told me all those things that happened so long ago," Gloria said to her friend.

"That I had forgotten. I repressed my memories."

Ned said, "How did they come back?"

Gloria answered. "We were talking about an article on the priest scandal, and about how some women, and men, remembered after many, many years things that had been done to them. Psychological explanations were given, don't ask me what. Anyway, suddenly Maddie just burst out crying."

"The floodgates opened, and I remembered. A little at first, then more and more."

It seemed to help that she could tell it all again to Gloria. Once she started, she didn't need much prompting from anyone. She seemed reluctant to pause when he turned over the cassette, and then she was off again.

Ned Bunting felt like Norman Mailer with all those tapes on which to base *The Executioner's Song*. How could he miss? This story could literally write itself. What else was *In Cold Blood,* literary granddaddy of reality as fiction? Faction. Ned Bunting would be the amanuensis of the victims of priestly predators. Gloria squeezed his arm three times during that sentence and gave him a hug when he was done.

"Logorrhea," he said diffidently.

"I always take paregoric."

When did he first see the personal connection with Gregory Barrett? Maybe he had tried to suppress that memory. The suggestion made Madeline Murphy's story seem less implausible. Ned had sent Barrett one of his stories after a program on Malamud, advising that if he liked Malamud he would like the enclosed. No response. Then there was a program on J. F. Powers. Ned had a story on parish bingo that owed a lot to St. Bavo's. He was sure it was his best to date. From Barrett he got a printed slip: We are not a publisher; we do not read unsolicited manuscripts. A variation on the printed slips Ned had been collecting for years. It was the handwritten addendum that made this one different. "Pretty bad." An enmity was born.

Whereas previously Gregory Barrett had been a genial voice expressing a love of literature, now he was a pompous ass who seemed to think his shapeless thoughts on the things he read could be of interest to anyone other than his psychiatrist. Or words to that effect. Ned printed it out and sent it off to Barrett, then suppressed all memory of him. Who cared about Barrett's opinion? Ned had been rejected by experts.

He filled two whole cassettes with Madeline's memories of then-Father Gregory Barrett. Madeline spoke in a dreamy voice, with her eyelids half closed, and a little smile that alternated with the frown that brought her brows into a chevron over her cute little nose.

"I spoke to his wife."

"Spoke to her?"

"I wanted to warn her. Imagine, being married to a man with that kind of past."

"You don't have to mess up his life, his family, just because of what he did to you." Even as he said it, he wanted it refuted.

"He denies anything happened."

Ned would have liked to feel more sympathy with Madeline. Even if you accepted the memory recovery stuff, didn't that argue for the reverse as well, just shutting things out? Or was that the theory Madeline's case was based on? Things suddenly came back after many years had passed. Remembering memories.

"Well, what do you think?" Gloria asked when they were alone.

"She must have been better-looking at sixteen."

"Oh, you." A dig in the ribs. "You will write the book, won't you?"

He patted his tape recorder, as if in promise. What would she say if she knew he had never published a word?

10

How deceiving looks could be, Marie Murkin mused. Put a presentable man into well-tailored clothes and send him over to the St. Hilary rectory and Marie Murkin would praise him to the skies. A serial murderer? But he had such gentle eyes. Bah. She really wasn't angry with herself. Of course she had known of men who left the priesthood, sometimes on the sly, sometimes with a certificate or whatever saying it was okay, and most of them got married, as often as not to a woman who had been a nun—but don't get her started on nuns. At the moment, Marie wanted to concentrate on the duplicity of the male.

Ned Bunting was another case. A fine figure of a man, always dressed to the nines, though what he did for a living not even Barbara had been able to find out. Her guess, and it was only a guess, was inherited money.

"Any more on the floozie?"

"Gloria Daley. Apparently a widow."

"Apparently?"

"She never properly registered in the parish. People seldom

do nowadays. They just keep shopping around. No collection envelopes, so who knows what they put in the basket? We get a lot of dollar bills at St. Bavo's, all folded up so maybe the usher will think it's more."

Marie knew all about such tricks. The empty envelope, or one filled with discount coupons. "I gather she lives alone."

"Very arty. Some of her paintings were on display in August at the parish picnic."

"Paintings of what?"

"Oh, they're not *of* anything. Art is about art." Barbara's voice had become a lazy drawl. "That's how she talks. And that is exactly what she said when people asked about her pictures."

"Sounds like a flake."

"Oh? She's home painting pictures and we're working our fingers to the bone, so who's nuts?"

"Barbara, if you ever retired they'd have to close St. Bavo's."

"Right after the funeral."

An hour later, there was a tap on the kitchen door and there was Ned Bunting, big as life. Marie banged her hip on the corner of the table in her haste to get to the door.

"Ned Bunting!"

"How on earth did you know my name?"

Marie had the door open. "Come into my kitchen, said the spider to the fly."

"I came to the back door because I didn't want to bother Father Dowling."

"You're out of luck if you want to see him. This is the day of his monthly retreat."

"But I want to see you."

She got him seated; she made tea; she cut him a large slice of her pineapple upside-down cake and then sat across from him.

"Why would you want to see me? No, go ahead, eat."

He had stopped a fork full of cake on its way to his mouth, and Marie wanted to see someone enjoy the food she prepared. God knows, Father Dowling would be content with graham crackers and milk. That was his idea of a treat. That and popcorn. Anyone can make popcorn.

"Mmmm. Delicious."

"You can take some with you when you go."

"But I just got here."

This visit would have been easier to handle if Marie hadn't had the persistent thought that Barbara was tuned in to the scene, monitoring her every move, listening to what she said. She remembered that imitation of Gloria Daley's drawl.

"I don't suppose you know I'm a writer."

"A writer."

"Let me tell you about my current plans. You know as well as I do the kind of pleasure the media have been taking in raking priests over the coals, all priests, because of a few bad apples."

Marie was nodding her head and tipping back and forth in her chair. She knew, she knew.

"My idea is that this story deserves more serious treatment, one that will put it into perspective. Why have I come to you? I want to give a sense of what the day-to-day life of a good priest is, the work he does, the long hours, the whole picture."

Thank God he had come to St. Hilary's. There were parishes where most of the work was farmed out to laypeople. What the priest did besides say Mass was hard to say. Marie had seen parish bulletins with rosters as long as the page, listing all the "ministers" of this and that. No wonder some priests got in trouble. Idle hands are the devil's workshop.

"You want a sketch of Father Dowling's day?"

"That's right."

So Marie gave him a portrait of the Curé d'Ars moved to Fox River. The man must sleep, but when, that was the question. He was still up when she went to bed and as often as not was already up when she came down to prepare breakfast.

"Not that he'll eat anything special. That cake? I made it three days ago. He had maybe a sliver. For him, that's pretty good."

"It's delicious. Does he pray a lot?"

"I don't spy on him, Ned."

She mentioned the study, and he asked if he could see it, so she took him down the hall. He put just the upper half of his body in the door and looked around at the books.

"Do I smell tobacco?"

"His pipe."

"He smokes?"

"Why not?"

"Maybe I won't mention that."

"No need to. It isn't that he couldn't stop in a minute. Is that a camera?"

Standing next to him, she was at eye level with the case that hung from his shoulder.

"A tape recorder."

"I hope it isn't on."

"I usually plug it in."

* * *

Two days later a photographer from the *Fox River Tribune* showed up at the rectory.

"We need a few photos to go with the story."

Father Dowling emerged from his study and came down the hallway toward Marie and the visitor. Suddenly the hall was filled with flashing light. The man had taken two pictures.

"What is this all about?"

Marie would have liked to flee, but the question was directed to her.

"He wants your picture."

"For the Ned Bunting story about you," the reporter explained. " 'Profile of a Faithful Priest.' "

"How could he write a story about me? I've never met him." The pastor turned slowly. "Marie?"

"It's a long story," she murmured.

"Not fifteen hundred words," said the photographer.

The photographer, Topolino, would have to settle for the shots he got of Father Dowling coming down the hall.

"I'd like to check some things in the story, Father. It's by a freelance . . ."

"There won't be any story if I can stop it."

"First Amendment, Father. First Amendment."

Father Dowling's call to Quirk, the editor, had no effect. The story would be run. No, the priest said, he didn't want to see it before it appeared.

"I didn't mean you could edit it, Father. Just a heads-up."

Listening on the kitchen extension, Marie knew she was in deep trouble. It was all Ned Bunting's fault. She had been Eve to his snake in the grass. She waited for the wrath of Father Dowling to fall on her, but minutes passed, then half an hour. She crept to the kitchen door and listened. No sound. She pushed it open slightly to see that the study door was closed. The silent treatment? Back in her kitchen she groaned. She infinitely preferred a scolding to the silent treatment.

What the *Tribune* called a profile of a faithful priest by Ned Bunting shook the even tenor of Roger Dowling's day. Since his assignment to St. Hilary's he had receded from public view, no longer part of the archdiocesan aparatchik, able to give his all to the demands of his parish. To call him or anyone else just doing his job "faithful" was about as flattering as it would be for a husband to be called that, or perhaps "nonadulterous." He didn't blame Marie Murkin as much as she deserved to be blamed, and for a time he hoped that the sheer illiteracy of the piece would rob it of any power to disturb his life. Unfortunately, it was the very awfulness of it that attracted.

"Could I speak to the faithful pastor of St. Hilary's?" One classmate after another called, asked this question, and then congratulated him for running that ad in the *Tribune*.

Roger took his punishment like a man, not least because it was undeserved. Beneath the kidding they detected that no one was more amused and bemused by the article than the Reverend Roger Dowling, the faithful pastor of St. Hilary's. It was the accompanying photographs that drew the most attention, though. In one, Father Dowling was coming down the hallway, a look of astonishment on his face. The other was a studio portrait taken while he was still on the archdiocesan marriage court.

"Is that your ordination picture, Roger?" His classmate Holt grinned when he said this.

He was almost sorry he hadn't let the photographer have his way and get some current shots.

"What can I say?" Marie said abjectly.

"It would be best if you took a vow of silence."

"He plans to write a book about the priest scandal."

"Good Lord."

"It's about time. And that was the point of the article, to show what most priests are like."

"I can't believe he could write a readable book."

"People eat up scandal, you know that."

"I was thinking of his prose."

"Well, you're a better judge of that than I am."

"Oh, I don't know. I had no idea you had become such a magnet for aspiring writers."

"I said I was sorry."

Ned Bunting called several times, but Marie told him it probably would be best not to talk to Father Dowling.

"What a response I've gotten," Ned enthused.

"That's his complaint."

"Of course, he's being modest."

"He commented on your style."

"Did he? Well, well. Just pass on my appreciation, Marie. I hope I haven't got you in trouble."

"Trouble? Me? By the way, who is that older woman I've seen you with at Mass?"

"Older?" He laughed, almost a giggle. "It's just that I seem much younger than I am."

"Hmph."

"Her name is Gloria, Gloria Daley."

Ned Bunting was in seventh heaven. After years of drought, his first published piece had caused a mild sensation. Thank God, he had Gloria with whom to savor this belated recognition.

"There should have been a picture of you as well," she said.

Ned would have accepted any terms Quirk of the *Tribune* had offered, short of asking that he use a pen name. All the years of dreaming, those awful times when he had paid through the nose for nothing, the demeaning interview with Zubiri at the writers' conference, faded into insignificance. He sought parallels in the life of other writers, those who after years of rejection had finally broken into print. Of course, his dream had been to write fiction, and this was a report on an actual person, but he had employed the fictional techniques he had learned, however imperfectly, dramatizing the life of the reclusive Roger Dowling.

"I'll bet Monsignor Sledz is eating his heart out," Gloria said. "Not that you could have made much of his day-to-day life."

Ned felt awash with magnanimity. His opponents of yore were now enveloped in the sense of triumph that suffused him.

"Ned, now you *have* to write that book."

A sobering reminder. It was one thing to put together a few pages from the conversation with Marie Murkin he had recorded, but a book suggested an extended effort, and in his heart of hearts the worm of doubt entered. When he compared the printed version of his story with the file on his computer, he realized that much editorial discretion had been exercised in preparing the printed version. He sought in vain for unaltered sentences from his original. He did not find the altered versions an improvement. There was a lesson there. The prospect of publication had made him docile to a fault. As long as his name appeared on the result, he would be satisfied. Not that he put it so baldly even to himself.

"We seldom run things by freelance writers," Quirk had said.

"This is special."

"Oh, we want it. Who helped you with it?"

"Helped me?"

"It reads as if it were translated from the Portuguese."

"I was trying for an impersonal style."

"We'll clean it up."

A writer with a record, anyone with a sense of self-esteem, would have reacted negatively to that condescension, but Ned had been ready to kiss the hand that edited his prose. In the event, the sentences Gloria singled out for praise had not figured in his original version. Prudence suggested silence. Praise had been so long coming, he was not likely to protest.

Then came the call from Henry Drummond.

"Who hired you to write that crap, the cardinal?"

This was the first sentence Ned heard when he answered the phone, and he didn't like the tone or the message. He hung up. Caller identification told him that the person who persisted in trying to get through to him was Henry Drummond. He called Gloria.

"Drummond's a crank. Maddie has told me all about him."

So Ned talked with Madeline.

"He's not interested in me at all, Ned. This whole scandal means nothing to him except that he was fired by the archdiocese and wants to give them as much trouble as he can."

"Fired?"

"He's an accountant."

It sounded like an indictable offense.

"He has been in contact with you?"

"On advice of counsel I have stopped taking his calls."

"Counsel."

"My lawyer."

"And who is that?"

"I just became his client. Tuttle. Of Tuttle and Tuttle."

Who is to say when the main chance may come? Tuttle had practiced law in several senses of the term, never getting very good at
it, but what he lacked in knowledge was more than made up for
by perseverance. He was on a mission from his father, the other
Tuttle in the name of the firm, currently playing a harp in the
next world. Tuttle's devotion to his paternal parent was Chinese
in its proportions. He did not have an effigy of his father before
which he burned incense, but a photograph of Tuttle père hung
on his office wall, and his apartment was filled with framed snap-
shots of the couple that had borne and raised and nurtured him.
When his mother died, his father redoubled his efforts to get
Tuttle settled in life. Through the long agony of law school, when
Tuttle had taken each course at least twice before achieving a
passing grade, through graduation and then the longer agony of
trying to pass the bar exams, his father had been his mainstay.
No doubt had ever crossed the paternal mind. Tuttle fed on his
father's trust. Finally, not without sleeves full of notes, he had
passed the bar exams. Like Moses viewing the promised land
but destined never to enter it, Tuttle senior almost immediately

went to his reward. The duplication of his name in the title of the firm was Tuttle's perpetual remembrance of the father who had never lost confidence in him.

A troubled life is not the worst preparation for the practice of law. Tuttle had learned to think that those who came to him—to him, the least of the local bar—had unstated reasons for their choice. So it had been with Gregory Barrett. One lead led to another, and before long Tuttle knew that his secretive client had once been a priest of the Chicago archdiocese. He had been laicized in an orderly way, nothing wrong there, and then had gone south to Cairo, where over time a small but prestigious involvement in public radio had begun. There seemed to be few books that Barrett had not read, and he had the charming faculty of liking most of them. His book chats were soon popular; the local station got him national syndication. Can any good come out of Cairo? Many thought so. It was pleasant to listen to his oral essays on the authors he had enjoyed, and not only the authors and their editors were appreciative. Eventually he was invited to relocate to Chicago, where an even wider audience for his program could be had.

So what was such a man doing seeking help from Tuttle? The question had dictated checking out Gregory Barrett—not the name he had used when he came to Tuttle's office. It was not long before Tuttle knew that the Madeline he had been asked to look into—there was no suggestion that the assignment was to dig up dirt on Barrett's nemesis—was pointing the finger, after all these years, at the onetime Father Barrett. The case was unique in the current burgeoning scandal. Barrett had been laicized for nearly a quarter of a century; he had a wife and family; he had built a small but prestigious career, translating his bookishness into a program with wide appeal.

No one could become even superficially interested in the local version of the clerical scandal without becoming aware of Henry Drummond. Tuttle's soul would not perhaps survive close scrutiny, but he found himself torn between seeking to represent Drummond and riding Madeline Murphy's complaints to profit and glory. As it happened, he went first to Drummond.

There are drinkers and drinkers, but it was hard to know into which category Henry Drummond fell. Tuttle came upon him in a place called the Montenegro Internet Café, where the aggrieved former employee of the archdiocese of Chicago was scanning a monitor with what might have been an eight-ounce glass of pure scotch at his elbow. He merely grunted when Tuttle tried to interrupt him. Then, like someone on a cell phone, Drummond began to talk. It was some time before Tuttle realized that his addressee was the universe or anyone within hearing range.

"Have you read this piece of crap?"

"I'd have to know more before I answered that."

Drummond swung in his chair, gripping its arms as if fearful of losing his balance, and sought some lens in his glasses that would enable him to see Tuttle clearly. "Who the hell are you?"

"Someone who has yet to read that piece of crap."

"Good man. I'll print it out."

As it happened, Tuttle had already read it. The article on Father Dowling did not read much better as a downloaded text than it had in the *Tribune*. Drummond sipped and watched Tuttle closely as he perused the pages.

"You see what they're doing, don't you?"

The words arrived on clouds of boozy breath, and Tuttle involuntarily backed away. "My name is Tuttle."

"And mine is Henry Drummond."

"I know that."

"But do you know that my life was ruined by the Archdiocese of Chicago? Do you know that in middle life I was put penniless on the streets under a cloud such that no one would dream of employing me? I have sought redress in the courts . . ."

"Who represents you?"

It was Drummond's turn to back away. He studied Tuttle, a frown coming and going on his brow, and then a smile. "You're a lawyer. I've seen you around the courthouse."

"No doubt." Tuttle adopted the expression of a man busy about many things. "Who has been representing you?"

"Misrepresenting, you mean."

"I meant your lawyer."

"So did I. I fired the bastard. I think he was in league with my enemies."

Tuttle said nothing. Conspiracies of this sort largely take place in the minds and imaginations of their supposed victims. It would be impossible to find Henry Drummond prepossessing, but then he had been put through the wringer in the past several years.

"Do you drink?" he suddenly demanded of Tuttle.

"No." Is there a secondary effect of liquor as well as of smoke? The fragrance of Henry Drummond's breath made abstinence seem overwhelmingly attractive.

"Good. Never trust a lawyer who drinks." Somehow the glass he held was empty, and he lifted it high, signaling the bartender. "But come, let us get out of traffic." Drummond rose and walked carefully among the empty tables and chairs to a corner table.

The sound of the chair on the granite floor when he pulled it free from the table caused him to cry out. He sat and put his face in his hands. He opened them, peekaboo, and said, "If they wanted to break me, all they would have to do is drag such chairs across such a floor. That sound pierces my soul."

Tuttle sat. "Fingernails on a blackboard."

"Not even close." He banged on the table. *Cameriere. Mosso. Garçon.*"

"The same?" asked a voice.

"Toujours la même chose. Yes, my good man."

A woman put a glass before him and glanced at Tuttle. "You want anything?"

"Not at the moment, no."

"He's a lawyer," Drummond said piously.

"Tell me about your case."

How lucid the man was when he got on his grievance. In his telling of it, the accusation against him, peculation, had never been documented. He was confronted with the charge, told that his employment was terminated, and, as he put it, was on the street. The matter received no publicity until Drummond decided to make it a cause célèbre, but the result had been simply to discredit himself. Since no public charge had been made against him, libel seemed out of the question. Drummond's lawyer had asked the archdiocese for a letter of recommendation. He received one—matter-of-fact, a simple recounting of his time with them, ending with the date of his resignation. No reason given. His lawyer advised him to use the letter and get another position. Drummond laughed, and his eyes narrowed in shrewdness. "They would do it by word of mouth, don't you see?

A call from a prospective employer, an ambiguous remark from my erstwhile boss, all of it beyond the reach of the law."

"What are you living on?" Drummond was well dressed, kempt, and thin—but then, his caloric intake was probably mainly liquid. He was clean shaven. Take away the smell of booze and he might have been a respectable accountant.

"Hope! And a little something from my father."

"Ah." A man who spoke well of his father was a man after Tuttle's own heart. "How much did you think of demanding from the archdiocese?"

"Money? It is not a question of money! It is they who think in terms of money, twisting a pardonable mistake in calculation into an effort to despoil the archdiocese. Nonsense."

The priest scandal had seemed to Drummond his great opportunity.

"Their main weapon does not even need stating. Enormous prestige locally. But that prestige has been wounded, mortally wounded. It is they who are in the dock now. It is time to strike."

"We must plan our strategy carefully."

Drummond did not object to the personal pronoun. Tuttle thought of asking for a retainer but decided to settle for a handshake.

"God bless you, Tuttle," Drummond called after him.

Covering his bets, he went next to Madeline Murphy.

"Have you read the piece by Ned Bunting?"

"I've met him," she said carefully.

How easily he gained entrance to the house. She was not alone. A sullen lad looked out from what must be the kitchen, chewing on a sandwich.

"This is my son, Marvin."

Tuttle was trying to remember whether she was married, not that marriage was any longer considered a must for parenthood. He doffed his tweed hat, and the boy disappeared. Tuttle sat and began to praise the article Ned Bunting had written.

"I couldn't read it. You understand."

"And now I suppose he will write about you."

"I suppose. He understands that it is not a question of money. Lawyers seem to think that money solves everything."

"They themselves get a good portion of the settlement, of course."

"Is that true?"

"I am a lawyer."

"A lawyer!"

"We are not all so bad."

"And why should I consider myself just one of an army of plaintiffs? My case is unique."

"Tell me how the memory came back to you."

"Oh, that was just a ruse. Do you think I could have forgotten a thing like that? I kept quiet about it, of course."

"That might weaken your case."

She smiled. "Oh, no. I always have Marvin."

Someone to fall back on in defeat? Marvin had once again appeared in the kitchen door. The lad seemed a slender reed to lean on.

"Marvin is his son, you see."

Tuttle's mind was not slow—when his own advantage was involved, he could think with astonishing rapidity—but now his mind seemed to slip into neutral. He looked at Madeline, at her sad, sweet, knowing smile. Over her shoulder, the slouching Marvin still chewed on his sandwich. The son of Gregory Barrett?

"We must hold that back, for maximum effect."

They shook hands solemnly. Before leaving he advised her to have nothing to do with Henry Drummond. No need for clients to meet one another.

"Perhaps you saw my story on Father Dowling in the *Tribune*?"

"You wrote that?" Gregory Barrett looked at his visitor. Ned Bunting seemed of average intelligence, was certainly of more than average height, and wore an expectant smile.

"It was a labor of love."

Good Lord. Someone should have translated it into English. "I know Father Dowling."

"I understand you were classmates."

"Did he tell you that?"

"Why would he? But you see the connection between what I wrote of him and what I could write about you. Schoolmates, for a time priests together, and then a parting of the ways . . ."

"You will write no story about me, Mr. Bunting."

"Yes. I will. The choice is whether I do it with or without your cooperation. Of course I know the charge that has been brought against you."

Once Gregory Barrett's life had been lived under the sign of Christian charity—every person was beloved of God and should be treated as such—but in recent years he had adopted the canons of civility as sufficient for his dealings with others. This had involved no outward change. In either case, striking a man would have been ruled out. When Madeline Murphy had made her accusation, he had felt a sudden surge of anger, but it had no target, certainly not that pathetic woman. He stood and for a moment was certain he would strike Bunting. What he did was come around his desk, take his visitor by the elbow, and escort him into the hallway. When he let go he gave a little push, and Ned Bunting staggered away, his expression one of disbelief. Then, noticing something over Barrett's shoulder, he reeled and crashed to the floor. Barrett turned to face Sinclair, the station manager.

"What's going on, Greg?"

"You saw what he did," Bunting cried from the floor. "He assaulted me, a writer!"

Sinclair laughed. "I saw you throw yourself down on the floor."

Bunting had a little trouble getting to his feet. He looked at Barrett as if seeking appropriate words and, finding none, glared at Sinclair. Then he was gone.

"What was that all about?"

"He wanted to write a story about me."

Sinclair's brows went up. "What's wrong with a little publicity?"

"Did you see that piece in the *Tribune* about the parish priest?"

"I couldn't read it."

"Now you have part of my reason for throwing him out."

Sinclair supplied the rest of the reason without saying it and laid his hand on Barrett's arm.

"What is your topic today?"

"Willa Cather. *Shadows on the Rock; Death Comes for the Archbishop.*"

"Sounds good."

It did, but the feeling that was usually his when he recorded his program did not accompany him to the studio. He loved Willa Cather; she had written two of the best Catholic novels in American literature but was not herself a Catholic. What would Willa Cather have thought of a man who left the priesthood? A man who had murderous thoughts about a would-be writer like Ned Bunting? Incompetent he might be, but the *Tribune* had run that piece on Roger. Imagine what he would do with Gregory Barrett.

The accusation by Madeline Murphy had the strange effect on Nancy and himself of returning them to the days when they had both changed their lives, marrying and going far from any reminders of what they had been, he a priest, she a nun. Over the years, the memories faded and it was as if they had never been otherwise than as they were. Then they had returned to the Chicago area, and within a year the accusation had come. It had begun when Madeline Murphy telephoned and talked with Nancy.

She told him of it, and they both verbally dismissed it, but how could Nancy fail to be affected by a call that accused her husband of taking advantage of a young parishioner long ago?

"I don't remember such a name."

He wanted to deny it, to declare his innocence, to assure

Nancy that he had never seduced anyone. That would have been absurd, though, and for the first time he saw the effect of such an accusation: Any denial conferred on it some kind of reality.

"Well, you can't remember them all." Nancy smiled and came into his arms. She was right. Humor was the only defense.

He prayed that the phone call would be a single event, some madwoman deriving satisfaction from seeing herself as a victim. Had he prayed so fervently in years? How had the woman chosen him to harass? There must be some connection between his priestly life and the girl. She knew that he had been a priest. Of course, there would be many who knew that. Amos Cadbury's suggestion that he talk with Roger Dowling was inspired.

"Of course I know Father Dowling," Gloria said in reply to Tuttle's question. "I'm surprised you do."

Almost as surprising was her knowing Tuttle, but Madeline had mentioned the lawyer, and Gloria wondered if he would like some paintings to hang in his office and managed to run into him at the courthouse. Now he had stopped by.

"My walls are filled with awards."

"I have some small ones."

She offered to come by his office to see which of her paintings might fit, but the suggestion filled him with alarm. It turned out that he was nagged by his secretary.

Gloria got to know him better. If nothing else, it might make Ned jealous.

"I'm full of surprises," Tuttle said in answer to her remark about his knowing Father Dowling. "The good father would like to meet our friend Madeline Murphy, and I want you to set it up."

"Meet with her?" Like Ned, Gloria had come to like Father Dowling—seen from the pews on a Sunday, that is. Of course, they were comparing him with Monsignor Sledz, "the martinet of St. Bavo's," in Ned's phrase, which sounded better than it meant because she wasn't all that sure of the meaning of "martinet." ("Some kind of bird?") Maddie's quarrel was with Gregory Barrett, but no doubt the clergy rallied around one of their own.

"Gloria, he may be the only one who gives a damn about her."

"Well, thanks a lot."

"He has talked with Gregory Barrett, sure. They were classmates back in the Ice Age. Maybe we shouldn't handicap priests, but if we did I'd put Dowling way out in front of those I know."

"Who's that in the car?"

"A friend of mine."

"He's asleep."

"He's a cop. Peanuts Pianone."

"Pianone!"

"The family's ambassador to the Fox River Police Department."

"That's nice."

"Peanuts is harmless. So what do you say? Do you talk to Madeline or do I?"

"Why didn't you just go ask her?"

Tuttle hesitated, about to lie. "I think this needs a woman's touch."

"I'll think about it."

"Time is of the essence."

It was going on noon. Ned would be coming by for lunch. "Call me in an hour or so."

"I'll come by."

"Call me first."

Tuttle hurried out to his car and hopped in, slamming the door. The Pianone ambassador slept on, but when the car lurched forward, so did he. Then the car went out of sight.

Ned didn't like the idea. "Madeline is putty in the hands of a priest," he said significantly.

"Ned! You know Father Dowling."

"Sure, and I thought I knew Monsignor Sledz."

"This is different."

"He'll try to talk her out of going after Barrett."

"What if he did? You have your story."

Ned frowned. "Quirk wants me to work with a reporter from the *Tribune*. A double byline."

"Did you tell him what the story is?"

Ned looked shrewd. "Of course not. They'd cut me out entirely if they had any inkling there's a child in the case."

Child. Gloria thought of Marvin. The son of a priest? Much as she liked Maddie, she found Marvin a little weird. What did he do all day while Madeline was at the library?

"He's pursuing his education," Maddie said, her tone defensive.

"At home?"

"By correspondence. On the computer. There are online universities."

Well, apparently she wanted to believe it. As far as Gloria could see, Marvin was a bum, prematurely retired in his midtwenties. Now he had taken an interest in his mother's grievance.

"You've told him about himself?"

Maddie's hesitation gave the answer to that question, but Marvin had told his mother she was crazy not to take the money offered to her by the archdiocese.

"He may be right."

"I thought you understood."

"Maddie, what is your best-case guess as to the outcome of all this?"

"Vindication!"

"You mean revenge?"

"Call it that if you like."

To Ned, Gloria said, "Sometimes I could kick myself for helping her remember her past."

"I wonder what else she's going to remember."

They were sitting after lunch in Gloria's studio, pictures in various stages of completion cluttering the area, the smell of turpentine and gesso and paint. She was back to oils, if only because they took longer, and her inventory was filling the house. Madeline had told her that Pasquali, the head librarian, thought that her exhibit had gone on long enough.

"Give me another week."

"Gloria, if it was up to me, they could stay there forever."

Maybe that was the solution. She would donate them to the library. Ned could write it up. They went together to the library. By agreement, they did not stop at the desk to talk to Maddie but went directly to Pasquali's office.

"This is Ned Bunting, Mr. Pasquali."

"Of the *Tribune*," Ned added.

Pasquali's wariness went. "What can I do for you?"

Gloria said, "It's about my paintings that have been on display here." The brightness dimmed. Apparently he had not made the connection. "I intend to donate them to the library."

"It will make a great little story," Ned said.

"You mean a permanent gift?"

"As an expression of gratitude for what libraries have meant to me in my life. Especially this branch."

"How do you spell your name?" Ned asked. It had been on the door and it was on a plaque on Pasquali's desk, but the librarian obligingly spelled it out for Ned. The prospect of publicity, of his name in the paper, had obviously driven out the negative judgment he had made of Gloria's paintings in telling Maddie he wanted them out of here.

"Those creeps looking at porn on our computers could paint as well as that," he had grumbled.

"I don't think you would want to hang any pictures they might paint."

Maddie had been proud enough of that retort to pass it on, but the sting had remained in Gloria's soul. Now her own vindication had come, with Pasquali babbling away into Ned's recorder. Ned had brought a camera as well, and he took a picture of the artist and benefactor at the side of the grateful future custodian of a dozen precious paintings by Gloria Daley.

Pasquali came out with Madeline and Ned Bunting, intent on giving Ned a tour of the place.

"Maybe a shot of the exhibit?" Ned suggested.

"Of course, of course."

Pasquali led them off to the little windowless lunchroom to which the paintings had been removed. Maddie heard him calling it a temporary home for the paintings while he decided on their permanent disposition. Madeline fluttered her fingers as they went by the desk and winked. In a few minutes, Gloria was back.

"Do you know where he put my paintings?"

"In the lunchroom."

"Ned gave him hell about that. Where can we talk?"

"The lunchroom?"

"Ugh."

"Can we go out for a smoke?"

In back of the building was a loading dock, and it was there that the addicted among the employees of the Benjamin Harrison branch of the Fox River library withdrew to smoke, in good weather and bad. They were more likely to die of pneumonia than of any ailment connected with smoking.

Gloria shook two cigarettes free and offered one to Madeline. "Father Dowling wants to meet you."

"What for?"

"Ned and I have been attending Mass at his parish. He's heard about your awful experience and wants to talk with you."

"It's a trick."

"I don't think so. No, I'm sure it isn't. Do you know what I think? He may be the only one who really gives a damn about you."

"Why should he?"

"Maddie, he's a priest. The kind of priest we used to know." That was a mistake, but Gloria hurried on. "A straight shooter."

They talked about it for three cigarettes apiece. Gloria was about to light a fourth when Madeline said, "Where?"

"Here? At the rectory? Your place?"

Having a priest come to the library was out of the question. Madeline was ashamed of the dirty old men who spent the day calling up pornographic sites on the bank of computers. At home was Marvin, presumably continuing his education in the privacy of his own bedroom. That left the rectory.

"I could go with you," Gloria offered.

Madeline found that tempting, but only momentarily.

"But I can tell him you're coming?" Gloria persisted.

"Gloria, I am perfectly capable of making arrangements myself."

That seemed unkind given their close friendship. Who else would have helped Madeline elicit the memories of events that had scarred her soul?

"I don't want Marvin to know," Madeline explained.

Madeline Murphy, occupation librarian, lived with her son, Marvin, in a small bungalow not far from Dirksen Boulevard in Fox River. Her day was spent chasing derelicts from the computers on which they called up pornographic sites. Unbathed, with open mouths, barnacles on the ship of decent society that provided gratis this opening into hell, they awaited their Dante. Her zeal often brought her on the carpet of the head librarian's office. Tetzel of the *Tribune* had written of the assault on the First Amendment in the branch library, ringing all the accepted changes on untrammeled liberty. He gave his reader to understand that wars had been fought to secure the right of derelicts to peruse pornography at public expense.

"They commandeer the computers. They sit there for hours," Madeline complained to Pasquali.

"I know, I know." He had once loved books and had become a librarian with the sense that the profession would connect him with the Bodleian, with the scriptoria of medieval monasteries, with the great library at Alexandria. Now he presided over a branch that contained few books even twenty-five years old, with shelf upon shelf of the ephemeral fiction called romances, carrying on a brisk trade in videos and rock music on disks, as well as large-print mysteries.

"I did not become a librarian in order to run a sex shop," Madeline said.

"Now, now. That is too strong."

"Would you want your wife to patronize this library?"

It was for Marvin she really feared. He had dropped out of high school with the intent of joining the navy and failed to pass the physical. There had been some months of desultory employment in various fast-food franchises. Fast food! The phrase had false Lenten connotations. Twice he had walked away in disgust from the smell of grease, the aroma of hamburgers and french fries, the dumbos who came and stared at the pictured offerings in an agony of indecision. Who could blame him?

They had sat and plotted, mother and son, on how he could earn his high school diploma without going back to school. There were promissory ads in books of matches. Nothing came of them. Still, years later, he lolled around the apartment during the day, at the keyboard of his computer. Her experience at work stirred her motherly concerns. She was what is called a single mother, a category that aimed at rationalizing the irregular. Marvin had never had a father to model himself after. It was Madeline's shame that for years she had been in doubt as to who his father was. In the past into which for years she had been reluctant to peer, there had been a sorority party, the house full of men, soft lights, strong drink, and pulsating music that stirred the loins. In some haze of warmth and momentary pain she had given herself to someone. She had, in the old joke, taken a chance on a mattress and lost by winning.

The advice she was given at Student Health was lofty and moralizing. She could not responsibly bear the child. Nor need she. Relief was just an operation away. Whence came her resistance to this compelling counsel? Her whole being revolted at the idea. Mingled with her shame was the wonder that within her a new life was forming. She thought of going to the Newman Club, certain she would get different advice there, but she could not risk being seen there. So she went to a church several blocks from campus and talked with a young assistant, Father Barrett.

Had she expected threats of divine retribution? She had come like the woman taken in adultery, but her reception had been biblical. His compassion in her time of need was balm to her soul. He arranged for her to go off where she could have her child. She could give it up for adoption.

But, as she had resisted abortion, so she resisted adoption. The baby she bore was hers, and she resolved to raise it. Father Barrett had supported her decision. Her aging parents gave financial help, so she could continue school and earn her library degree. Did they believe her story that she had assumed the care of a child born of a straying sorority sister? In any case, they did not question it—but neither of her parents had ever seen Marvin.

She lied to her parents, and she lied to Marvin when inevitably he asked about his father. By then she had supplied herself with photographs from a garage sale: The young sailor smiling into the camera, his hat at a jaunty angle, was on her dresser for years, then transferred to a prominent place in the living room. She invented a heroic death for Marvin's putative father. Eventually he wanted to see the medals, the discharge papers, other photographs. Alas, she had given them into her parents' keeping, and in the confusion after their deaths—an accident on 101 near

Santa Barbara in which eight others had lost their lives—their effects were dispersed. The imaginary had become so vivid to her that she was almost surprised by Marvin's skepticism.

"Sometimes I think I was just left on your doorstep."

Sometimes she wished she had settled for such a simple explanation.

The photograph of the unknown sailor was behind Marvin's attempt to enlist in the navy.

She met Gloria when Pasquali asked her to accommodate the local artist who was offering to lend some of her paintings for display in the library. They hit it off immediately.

"I always wanted to paint myself."

"Don't."

"Why not?"

"There are too many of us already."

The paintings Gloria brought were certainly colorful. Madeline supposed they were abstract. After hours of indecision, they hung the paintings in various places, not wanting to group them. Seen side by side, they seemed to resemble one another too much.

"You certainly love yellow,"

"The color of cowardice."

Gloria did not want her photograph displayed along with her paintings. Instead, she offered a self-portrait. Madeline studied it.

"I'm in there someplace. Let me take you to dinner."

This was an unexpected pleasure. Madeline's life had become a parody of itself. Daytime in the library; after work, home to fuss over Marvin. When he was younger, there had been visits to museums, to the zoo, now and then a movie, but that was all behind them now. For Marvin, weekends meant hours and hours before the television watching sports—golf, basketball, football, hockey, it didn't matter, any contest could mesmerize him. He drank beer as he watched. Meanwhile, she sat in her rocker in the kitchen reading the kind of book that had drawn her into the library work and listening to NPR and the delightful program called *End Notes*.

That first time, she and Madeline had gone to a small trattoria where Gloria was obviously well known. Madeline let Gloria order for her. It was almost like a date. Madeline couldn't get enough of it when Gloria began talking about her husband.

"Gone to God, at least I hope so. He was killed in Iraq."

"Then we have that in common."

"You lost your husband?"

"He was in the navy."

"What I think now is, what if I had gotten pregnant."

"I did."

"Really."

So she told Gloria about Marvin, an account that bore as little resemblance to her son as Gloria's self-portrait did to her. It turned out that they had NPR in common.

"I have it on all day. Flaky liberals, most of them. It brings back my youth," Gloria said.

"I suppose you listen to *End Notes*?"

"Oh, that voice!" Gloria shivered and squeezed her eyes shut.

"I know him."

"You do!"

"Well, I did. A long time ago, when he was a priest."

Gloria sat back. "I knew you were Catholic."

"But I'm not. Not anymore."

"Wait until you see my favorite usher." Her brows danced. Honestly, she was so much fun to be with.

When Gloria came to the house and met Marvin, she flirted with him shamelessly. He loved it, his chest expanding like a pouter pigeon's under her flattery. How had Madeline's memories of Father Barrett fused with all the publicity about wayward priests?

"I lied about my sailor, Gloria."

"You weren't married?"

"Priests can't marry."

How easy it had been to say and how impossible to take back, particularly when Gloria was so excited about it. They talked for hours, and Madeline just nodded when Gloria attributed to her the business about suppressed memories. She agreed to write the letter to Mr. Barfield, the archdiocesan lawyer whose name figured in local stories about accused priests. The worst thing had been to telephone Barrett at home, but by then Madeline almost believed the story herself.

Madeline did go to church at St. Bavo's, where Gloria nudged her arm when the tall, imperious usher strutted up and down the aisle. Then she met Ned Bunting at Gloria's.

"I'm a writer," he had told her.

"Art has brought us together," Gloria simpered.

On that occasion, Madeline told herself that Gloria was just being flirty, as she had been with Marvin, but she found it hard not to resent Ned Bunting a little.

"So who's your squeeze, Madeline? The four of us could go out."

"Oh, there's no one in particular."

There had been no one all her life long. Once burned, twice shy.

"Just so it isn't Gregory Barrett." Gloria's eyes widened.

"That bastard," Ned said. "I sent him a story, and he sent it back with a nasty crack." He seemed about to say more but didn't.

"Maybe he isn't all he's cracked up to be. Madeline knew him when he was a priest."

"You did!"

"It's a long story."

The story developed over several occasions. It seemed a dreamlike sequence, the movement from talking with Gloria to accusing the archdiocese of letting a predator like Gregory Barrett loose on innocent young women. Lawyers had come to her, suggesting that her grievances could be answered with money. Madeline affected shock. How could she have sustained the story without Gloria's support? Ned, it turned out, was writing a book on the clerical scandals that were rocking the Church. Madeline was impressed when his article on Father Dowling appeared, despite the terrible job of editing. It was to Gloria that she had first confided—obliquely, not quite saying it outright—that Gregory Barrett was Marvin's father.

"Good God. You have to tell Ned."

Madeline panicked. After all, Ned was writing a book. With great reluctance she allowed herself to be interviewed by him, again and again, his tape recorder going. He seemed reassured, more than anything else, by the fuzziness of her memories. He explained the theory of repressed memory to her. It had become a commonplace. Under his urging, the past lost its vagueness. She told him how Father Barrett had arranged for her to have her child.

It angered Ned that when Barrett had left the priesthood he had not married Madeline. "Ran off with a nun, of course."

"I didn't know that," Madeline said.

Gloria told Ned about the photograph of the sailor in Madeline's living room and about the garage sale.

"I had to provide Marvin with a father," Madeline explained.

"Oh, you poor thing." Gloria took her in a plush embrace. How good it was after all these years to feel again the sympathy and compassion she had felt when she talked with Father Barrett.

Ned thought he was introducing her to the funny little lawyer in the tweed hat, Tuttle, describing him as his collaborator.

"You know him?" she asked.

Tuttle had looked Ned up, praised his account of Father Dowling, and given Ned his business card.

"I've told him everything, Madeline," Ned said.

"Everything."

"About Marvin's father."

"She wouldn't give her name," Marie said. "She just wanted to know if the priest would be home this afternoon."

"And you told her yes."

"No, I told her you had joined the foreign missions and were now in Nigeria."

Marie stomped back to her kitchen. She did not look kindly on anonymous visitors, unless they were drop-ins, and then she would quiz them before letting them see the pastor.

Father Dowling assumed it was Madeline Murphy. Tuttle had called to say that he had set the ball rolling, and Roger Dowling felt something of the unease Amos Cadbury did at this suggestion of collaboration. Still, when he had formed the resolution of seeing the woman who had made such serious charges against Gregory Barrett, he could think of no one other than Tuttle through whom he could broach the matter. He could simply have found out her address or where she worked and shown up, but he wanted some assurance that she was receptive to a meeting.

He closed his breviary on his finger and shut his eyes. *Veni sancte spiritus.* It was an occupational hazard to make prayer so routine it ceased to be prayer. "My words fly up, my thoughts remain below. Words without thoughts never to heaven go." It was no pro forma prayer he prayed now, asking for the grace to handle the situation well. Whatever the situation was.

When Gregory Barrett had first come to him, he had accepted his classmate's assurance that the charges against him were fantastic and that he had no memory whatsoever of his accuser. It was ironic that a man who had left the priesthood and had been living a useful, indeed successful, life since should be swept up in the current scandals. A first anomaly of the case was that the accuser did not agree to be a recipient of the archdiocesan settlement with victims of clerical abuse. Barrett's going to Tuttle when he was already a client of Amos Cadbury had seemed a faux pas, but the little lawyer had discovered things that had prompted Barrett to remember his accuser. The help he had given her when she came to him in trouble was just what a priest should have done, even though, in the present atmosphere, such pastoral help could be made to seem ominous: He had smoothed the way for her when she decided to have her baby, and when she changed her mind about giving it up for adoption, he had supported her decision. The woman's further claim that Barrett was the father of her child had changed everything, though. Barrett might have forgotten the help he had given a troubled young woman years ago, but he could scarcely have forgotten that he was a father. Roger Dowling believed his classmate's denial, even as he sympathized with Barrett's anguish at having to deny such a thing.

He heard the front doorbell and then the passage of Marie Murkin down the hall to answer it. He could hear two voices, one the businesslike voice of Marie, another muted, diffident. Then Marie opened the door, and the woman appeared beside her.

Father Dowling rose. "It is so good of you to come."

"I was told you wanted to see me."

"As I do, as I do. Please come in and sit down. Would you care for anything, coffee, tea?"

"I would like some water."

Marie nodded and withdrew. The silence was not uncomfortable as they waited for her to return with the water.

Madeline Murphy looked around the room and smiled. "I am a librarian."

"At the Benjamin Harrison branch."

"I have been there over twenty years."

"So you must like it."

"I do. Not that I have any alternative. It's the one thing I'm trained to do. Have you been there?"

"The Benjamin Harrison branch? No."

"You don't look as if you need any books. Not that the frothy stuff we feature would interest you. Do you know we don't even have a complete set of Dickens? Not that it matters, Nobody asks for him."

"And what is popular?"

"Movies on video and CD. Music discs. The computer." She shuddered. "Our branch has become a haven for derelicts. They commandeer the computers and spend hours looking at garbage."

"And you yourself love Dickens?"

"Just recently I read *The Pickwick Papers*. I thought I was rereading it, but if I ever had read it I had forgotten."

"Memory is a strange faculty."

"I know why you want to talk to me."

"Good. I should tell you that Gregory Barrett was a classmate of mine. When I saw him recently I realized I hadn't seen him since he left the priesthood."

"He was a priest when I knew him."

"Tell me about that."

"I think you already know."

"Only what others have said. You should know that my desire to see you is completely unofficial. Gregory Barrett does not know you're here, either."

"I wouldn't care if he did."

"Did you ever consider talking with him?"

"What would be the point?"

"Each of you might remember things. He said he had no memory of you until the record of your bearing your child connected him to you. He remembers now."

"He should."

"How old is your son?"

"Twenty-four."

"What does he think of all this publicity?"

"What I would think if I were he, I suppose."

"Tell me, what brought all these things back to you? For Barrett, it was the records. They make it clear that he sponsored you at the place where you had your baby and supported your decision to keep your son."

"That's true."

"And you had forgotten it?"

"If he could, why couldn't I?"

"And now you have both remembered."

"Does he admit that he is the father of my child?"

"No. But neither admission nor denial matters anymore."

"What do you mean?"

"If the charge were simply that he had acted improperly with you, it would be your word against his. If he denied it. Now all that has changed. Now we can be certain whether he is the father. There are tests . . ."

Her eyes widened. "Is that why you asked me here? Is that what you want me to do?"

"What I might want or not want doesn't matter. No, my interest is you."

She sat regarding him in silence, wary, curious, perhaps a gleam of trust.

"Let me tell you how all this seems to an old pastor."

He spoke softly, finding the words easily, not looking at her but, as it were, consulting the spines of the books he stared at without seeing. What must it be like for a woman who had kept and raised her child suddenly to remember something that put her in a very bad light? Oh, times have changed, of course. Statistics tell us of the number of children born of unmarried mothers. He doubted that she considered herself like one of those. "I am sure you thought of what you had done as a sin."

"Yes, I did."

"Did you confess it?"

"How could I go to another priest after . . ."

"You have come to me."

"This is different."

"One priest is very much like another."

"Not in my experience."

"If you had come to me as you did to Gregory Barrett, I hope I would have done what he did. Thank God you had your baby."

"I do. He is all I have."

"Have you raised him Catholic?"

"I stopped all that."

"To punish God?"

"What has God ever done for me?"

"What he did for all of us. He died for our sins so that we could put them behind us. You believed that once, didn't you?" She nodded. "I wonder what your son thinks life is all about."

She smiled. "Some friends of mine have been attending your Mass. I can see why."

"I won't say that I would like to be your friend. The best friend you can have is God."

She had sat there, holding the glass of water Marie had given her, not tasting it. "You're trying to trick me, aren't you?"

"God forgive me if I am. I think that what you really want is for a mistake you made long ago to stop being a mistake. Your son is not a mistake. What is his name?"

"Marvin."

"Is he baptized?"

She hesitated. "I did it myself."

"And you knew how to do it?"

"Yes."

"Does he know?"

"I never told him."

"Yet you knew why you baptized him. Don't you think he has a right to know? I wish I could talk to him."

"And turn him against me?"

"Quite the opposite. He should know what a wonderful mother he has."

"Thank you." Her eyes were moist now, and she took a sip of water.

"I hope he understands the sacrifices you've made for him."

"I don't know what he understands."

"He must understand that. And it is important that he does, whatever lies ahead. If your accusation proves true, as now it could well do, you will want your son firmly at your side. You will be subjected to all kinds of publicity."

"I don't want publicity."

"And you didn't want money, either."

"No!"

"It was when I heard that you had refused money that I wanted to meet you."

"I am not going to take back what I have said about Father Barrett."

"Have I asked you to?"

"So why did you want to see me?"

"I've been trying to explain."

"So I could go to confession?"

"That's up to you. I would like you to remove any barriers there are between you and God."

"I'll think about it."

"Good. And I'll pray about it. Maybe you could come to Mass here with those friends of yours."

"Maybe."

He stood, and she seemed almost surprised that it was over. He took the glass from her.

"I will think about it."

"Come back and see me, whatever you decide."

He went with her to the front door and watched her go out to her car. He was filled with a sense of inadequacy. Gregory Barrett would survive what lay ahead, he was sure of that, but what did that poor woman have but her son? And some friends who had come to Mass at St. Hilary's.

Hell hath no fury like a writer scorned. Ned Bunting was furious at the treatment he had received when he visited the cultivated voice of *End Notes*. The bum's rush. It occurred to him that the *Tribune* would be interested in the way one of its writers had been treated.

"It happens all the time," Quirk told him. "Don't call yourself one of our writers, by the way."

"But my piece on Father Dowling . . ."

"Well, we all make mistakes. I should have had someone put that into better shape."

"Listen, I have a real scoop."

"A piece on the housekeeper at St. Hilary's?"

It was all Ned could do not to blurt out that Gregory Barrett was the father of the child borne by the woman who had accused him of sexual misconduct. Here was proof positive of her charge. But if he told Quirk, he would be giving away the story. His dream of being a published writer would be nipped in the bud.

"And if I write the story and give it to him, he would steal it," he said to Gloria later.

"So keep it for your book. That was the original idea, wasn't it? Write that book and publish it and no one can steal it from you."

He was the victim of his own bragging. Apparently Gloria believed that he had written much already, meaning published much. She had asked him why none of his books were at the Benjamin Harrison branch of the Fox River library. Various answers occurred to him. Censorship? No, she would tell him about Madeline's complaints that the branch was a conduit of pornography.

"This will be the first book I publish under my own name," he said, treading a fine line between fact and fiction.

"Ned, I want to see some of your work."

So he picked up in a used bookstore a novel by an unknown writer and gave it to her as his own.

"Why Harry Austin?"

"Why not? A pen name can be anything."

"I don't understand why a man of your ambition would publish something under a phony name."

"Wait until you read the book."

So he was left with his dilemma. He had a bombshell of a revelation to make about Gregory Barrett, and he had no way to make it public. It was all very well for Gloria to tell him to write a book. Did she think a chapter on Father Dowling and another with the great revelation about Barrett's fathering Madeline's child would make a book? Meanwhile, the clerical scandal, far from dying out, seemed to be spreading across the country. Column after column in newspapers was filled with juicy reports on the dreadful things the Catholic clergy had been up to— Catholic as well as secular papers. Were Catholic publications his hope? Some of them salivated over the scandals even more than their secular counterparts, perhaps seeing them as vindication of their own misgivings about the direction the Church had taken since Vatican II. He went down to the Benjamin Harrison branch to do some research, and Madeline put him onto an appropriate volume. He told her what he was after.

"I'm not sure I want you to write about it, Ned."

He turned to her with narrowed eyes. "Did they get to you?"

"What do you mean?"

"I suppose they offered more money."

She stepped back, really steamed. "I'll try to forget you said that."

Ned tried to soothe her. He did not want the heroine of his story to be angry with him. Of course, given what Tuttle had confided in him, it no longer mattered what Madeline thought. He didn't need her permission to go ahead. Still, he would prefer to have her as his ally, rather than the victim this time of an intrepid writer who followed the truth wherever it led him.

"They will try, you know."

"I am thinking of myself. And of Marvin."

Ned nodded. "I can see that. Well, there's no harm in just making a few inquiries."

He took the reference book *LMP—Literary Market Place—* to a table and opened it to the index. An overpowering aroma of body odor drifted from the far end of the table, where a disheveled man was sleeping. Ned took his book and looked for a more antiseptic place to consult it. Suddenly it seemed to him that most of the clients of the library were derelicts. They were sleeping at tables, lounging in reading chairs, slavering over the wares they brought up on the bank of computers that they had commandeered. Good God, what a place. How could Madeline stand to work here? She had sought support from the Library Association in her campaign to have pornography blocked on the library computers; they sent her a stinging letter, recounting their long fight against censorship. Better that she should be angry at them than at him.

"Madeline called to tell me you were at the library today," Gloria said that night. They were having *risotto con funghi e piselli* at the Boca della Verità, a little Italian restaurant that had hung several of Gloria's paintings.

"What a dump that library is."

"She's having second thoughts, Ned. Maybe we should think of some other subject for you to write about."

Ned sipped his wine and stirred his risotto with a fork, causing steam to rise from it. "She got mad when I asked her if they had gotten to her."

"I think seeing Father Dowling has something to do with it."

"Dowling!"

"Tuttle arranged for her to go to the St. Hilary's rectory."

Ned sat back to let his risotto cool. He had burned his mouth with it, and a quick sip of wine had done little to put out the fire. "So that's their game."

"Oh, I can see her point, Ned. The truth is, I've been having second thoughts myself. Would any of this have come up if I hadn't urged Maddie to dredge up her past?"

"Her past? Marvin is very much in the present." The thought of Madeline's son was not encouraging. He was not, in a word Ned was seeking opportunities to use this week, a prepossessing figure. On the other hand, he seemed a poster child against impregnating young women and leaving them with the results of their folly.

"It doesn't put her in a very good light."

Was everyone against him? Well, he would fight on alone if necessary. When he left the library, he had gone home and shot off letters to the *Wanderer* and the *National Catholic Reporter*, enigmatically suggesting that he had a story they would certainly want to run. A new wrinkle on the clerical scandals.

"I wonder if Marvin hasn't been pointing that out to her."

Ah. If Marvin was the problem, he would address it head on.

So it was that on the following day, after Madeline had gone off to the library, Ned Bunting rang the bell of her front door. From what he had heard, Marvin was sure to be home. Parked down the street, waiting for Madeline to leave the house, he had seen no sign of Marvin up and about. He banged on the door and rang the bell insistently, but there was no answer. He went around the house to find the pajamaed Marvin sitting in the little patio, his hair wild on his head, a cup of coffee before him.

He looked at Ned with puffy eyes. "She's not here. She's gone to work."

"Is there any more coffee?"

"In the kitchen."

Ned went into the kitchen and poured a cup of coffee. Since he was inside, he made a quick inspection of the house. With the exception of the room that must be Marvin's, the house was neat as a pin. A paragraph formed in his mind. Abandoned mother provides ideal domestic setting for herself and her son . . .

Outside, he joined Marvin at the metal table. The chair was chill on his bottom. Marvin sat in sunlight, so his chair must have been warm when he sank into it.

"We're making progress, Marvin. I'm sure your mother has kept you informed."

Marvin gave an impatient toss of his head. "That's all crap."

Ned drank some coffee. It was delicious, obviously made by Madeline, for herself and her bewildered son. The paragraph grew.

"Vindication is not crap, Marvin."

"Look, my father was a sailor. I don't know where all this stuff about the priest came from. She never mentioned it to me. Her stories were all about my father the sailor. There are photographs in the living room." Marvin sat forward, fully awake now.

"Do you know his son had the guts to call me up and suggest we get together?"

"His son?" The sailor's? There wasn't any sailor, Ned knew.

"Thomas Barrett."

"He called you!"

"I told him I was too busy. So he threatened me."

Ned sat forward. "What did he say?"

"DNA."

"DNA?"

"What the hell does that mean?"

"As you say, it was a threat. They're getting worried."

"He asked about you, too. What have you written, anyway?"

"About your mother?"

"Don't write about her, understand? Don't. What good can it do her? She could have had a pile of money and she said no. That sounds crazy, but I admire her for it. It isn't as if we're independently wealthy." He tried to laugh and settled for coffee instead.

"She didn't take the money because then no one would have known . . ."

"And you think everyone should know? I mean it, Ned Bunting. Get interested in something else."

"The Barrett boy got you worried?"

"Oh, I calmed him down. I told him we were on the same page."

Madeline wanted out, Gloria had cooled on the project, and now Marvin was giving him orders as to what he could write. Ned Bunting was damned if he would sit still for that. He stood. "The First Amendment is a powerful weapon, Marvin. I will write what I write."

It wasn't a bad line to leave on. He executed an almost military about-face and went out to his car. But his zeal had thinned. For a week and more he had felt like the paladin of the downtrodden, the Upton Sinclair of the victims of priestly abuse. Gloria had encouraged him. His story about Father Dowling, a first salvo in his project, had gained notoriety, and then had come the revelation about Madeline's child. Now everyone seemed to be deserting him. He was treated with disdain by the likes of Quirk and Gregory Barrett. Must he give it all up? And for what? His writing aspirations had never materialized. Even Monsignor Sledz had ridiculed him. But by God, facts were facts, and no matter what anyone thought, friend or foe, he would go forward.

When Tuttle showed up at the studio, Gregory Barrett's first impulse was to get him out of there in the way he had Ned Bunting. Whatever persona he had developed through his program had been enhanced when he moved back to the Chicago area, and such visitors struck a discordant note. He took the little lawyer out to a bar, where Tuttle ordered root beer.

The bartender stared at him. "How about O'Doul's?"

"You're the boss. I usually have A&W."

Gregory ordered a scotch and water and began to explain why he had called himself William Arancia when he came to Tuttle's office.

Tuttle displayed a palm. "Think nothing of it. It happens all the time. Clients often say they have come because they're worried about someone else."

Barrett took little comfort in being classified among dissembling clients. How he regretted having gone to Tuttle at all. What would Amos Cadbury say if he knew he had consulted another lawyer? Not that it was easy to see the patrician Cadbury and Tuttle as members of the same profession.

"I should tell you that Amos Cadbury has agreed to represent me. At the request of the archdiocese."

Tuttle nodded, as if in approval. "Amos Cadbury."

"So if we can settle now . . ."

"But you haven't heard what I've learned."

Barrett considered his drink, where ice cubes jostled and pinged. Do not ask for whom the bell tolls. "I'm listening."

Once Tuttle began, Barrett suggested that they move to a table away from the bartender. In the shadow created by the brim of his absurd tweed hat, the little lawyer smiled. They settled at a table, more lawyer and client than ever. During the narrative, Barrett concentrated on the unlit candle on the table between them, a votive light whose flame might have warded off evil. The tiny wick was bent, and he had trouble lighting it with his cigarette lighter. Since he had it out, he lit a cigarette as well.

The knowing vulgar voice went on, undistracted by these movements. "So there is a record of your knowing her back then."

The theory of repressed or at least forgotten memory gained plausibility as Barrett felt the shards of the past rise within him. A troubled girl had decided to bear her child, and he himself had done the right thing. Of course he had arranged for her to have her baby.

"She has told others that the child is yours."

He simply dipped his chin and looked into the shadowed face.

"There are records of what you did."

Records that would redound to his credit, except with the more rabidly prochoice. It occurred to him that Amos Cadbury would certainly approve of what he had done, but to Cadbury he had denied ever knowing the woman. His denial had been solidly based on the fact that he did not remember her. How could he be expected to remember everyone he had encountered in his life as a priest?

"You say she has said this to others?"

"And to me. Of course I wanted to talk with her."

"What is she like?"

"A bit of a fruitcake. She works in a library. Bookish. She lives alone with her son. It was hearing your program that brought it all back."

"A son."

"She kept the baby. The plan was to give it up for adoption, but . . ."

"I remember." He did remember now.

Tuttle lifted his bottle and almost immediately put it down. "This is beer."

"A nonalcoholic beer."

"Ugh." Barrett himself drank as if from real need. His companion was a menace now, armed with this seemingly damning information from the past. "As you say, there will be records."

"I will look them up," Tuttle stated.

"Don't!" The word flew from his mouth. Checking the record of that pregnancy and birth would lend credence to the woman's absurd accusation.

"Others will check as well."

"Who?"

"Anyone can hire a lawyer."

"Who else has she told?"

"A man named Ned Bunting."

"My God."

"You know him?"

"He wrote that article about Roger Dowling." Tuttle seemed surprised that he knew this. "Roger Dowling and I were classmates."

"You were?"

"I have talked with him about this. Before I went to you. Tuttle, I will be frank. Amos Cadbury is no doubt a distinguished lawyer."

"The best."

"He clearly finds all this distasteful. He is an exemplary layman, but one doesn't have to be that to lament the kinds of stories that have become prevalent about priests preying on the faithful. He said what is doubtless true, that it is hard to prove a negative. My simple denial is just what would be expected. I went to you because I had been told . . ."

"That I am no Amos Cadbury."

"I wanted to know what I could about the person saying such things about me."

"You came to the right man."

"I wish to God I hadn't."

"If I were you, I would thank God that I did. What would you do if all this were simply sprung on you, records produced, the boy brought forward, and you unprepared?"

Barrett sank back in his chair. This was the worst conversation he'd had since he talked with Hennessy, the auxiliary bishop, and applied for laicization. The process was still more or less routine in those days.

"It goes more quickly when a marriage has already been entered into," Hennessy had said.

How do you tell an auxiliary bishop of the Archdiocese of Chicago that you have not broken your promise of celibacy? And he hadn't. He and Nancy had talked, walking in the evening on the playground of the parish school, two young people suddenly wanting to get out of the lives they led. This desire had grown because of their talks. Once he had put his arm around her and tugged her to him, but that was the extent of it. He had told Hennessy the truth, as he had to Roger Dowling, and Dowling at least seemed to believe him. How often in the years since had he and Nancy marveled at the innocence of those conversations when it became clear that the decisions they were about to make were a single decision, a joint one, a promise of a future together. And so it had turned out. But even Nancy had been shaken when that woman telephoned her and made her accusation.

"Does that sound like the man who took you for evening walks on the parish playground?" Barrett asked his wife.

She squeezed his hand, her doubts, if doubts they had been, gone. "But what can you do?"

"I suppose I could wish that she would let the archdiocese buy her off. It would be blackmail, but maybe that would be an end of it."

"I think she wants publicity more than money."

The accusation would have been bad enough at any time, but now when day after day stories appeared about what priests had done, stories that could not be doubted, that were in many cases acknowledged by the accused, he would seem merely one of a platoon of wayward clerics. How many had at first denied what was later proven of them? On the other hand, there was the case of Cardinal Bernadin, who had been accused by a young man of inappropriate sexual behavior when he was in Cincinnati. He had denied it calmly and met with the young man, and eventually the charge was withdrawn, admitted to be the product of a mind stirred by all the talk of repressed memory; for a time the man actually believed that he had some kind of affair with Bernadin. The upshot had given a tremendous lift to Bernadin's reputation. His meeting with the young man, like the pope's visit to the one who had tried to assassinate him, was a vivid example of Christian forgiveness.

He must meet this woman. It looked cowardly to screen himself from her with lawyers and inquiries into her life. How could she look him in the eye and make that accusation? He was on the verge of expressing this resolve to Tuttle, but that would be ridiculous. From now on it must be between him and Madeline Murphy.

"My secretary is typing all this up for you."

"Good."

"I will let you know what records there are of her giving birth—"

"No. Let's drop it here."

"Drop it? That makes it sound as if it is simply up to us."

Us. How the pronoun seared his soul. But the only way he could rid himself of Tuttle was to confront his accuser and persuade her to withdraw her charges.

Tuttle stood and picked up the bottle from which he had not drunk. He shook his head, adjusted his hat and turned away, then stopped. He came back to the table.

"Do you know Ned Bunting personally?"

"Why do you ask?"

"Avoid him. He's trouble."

21

Many of those Roger Dowling had known when he worked in the archdiocesan marriage court had gone on to the greater things that had been thought to be in store for him as well. First they had been auxiliaries, then got dioceses of their own, lifting into a clerical stratosphere that made it unlikely he would encounter them in his daily work as pastor of St. Hilary's. An exception was old Bishop Hennessy, already at that time one of the senior auxiliary bishops in the archdiocese and more than content to remain.

"Leave Chicago? Do you know the legend on the gates of Amalfi? When Amalfitani enter heaven, they have the sense of coming home. That is how I feel about Chicago. Can you see me as the ordinary of Boise?"

"I can't see you as ordinary anywhere."

As he did once a month at least, Roger was visiting Hennessy in his retirement. The now elderly bishop had resisted entering a retirement home and was now the chaplain for a house of Poor Clares.

"They are saints, Roger. This is the kind of place one wants to prepare for death in."

"I feel the same about St. Hilary's. Not that we have many saints there."

Hennessy loved to hear about Roger's parish and could not get enough of stories about Marie Murkin. "I wish I'd had sense enough to do what you did, Roger."

"It was done for me, Bishop."

Hennessy's ring had been given him by Pope John Paul II when he was consecrated, a ring identical to the pope's. The episcopal hand now held a cigar, an indulgence encouraged by the nuns.

"I think they fear I'll get religion."

Even so, they sat in the courtyard of the convent so that the cigar smoke would drift away in the April air. Inevitably they talked of the burgeoning clerical scandals.

"Cardinal Law has become a monster in the press, Roger, but I understand the man. When a scandal happens in a family, the impulse is to keep it quiet. Is that ignoble?"

It was a generous estimate, and would have been more deserved if the cardinal had not simply reassigned priests whose conduct warranted punishment rather than another parish. Hennessy had been the auxiliary in charge of laicization when requests had been in their flood.

"Of course, I was criticized for making it too easy for men to leave, but what was the alternative? Send them off to a monastery to think it over? Many of them were already involved with women. Even when they weren't, I came to see that by the time they came to me their minds were made up. So let those go who wanted to go. Delaying them might have led to scandal. Now I wish that more had gone, these poor devils we're reading about now."

"They couldn't do legitimately what they're accused of even if they were out of the priesthood."

"True. Yet dropping celibacy is the only solution some have. That's like making polygamy the remedy for adultery."

Roger laughed, however much the analogy limped. "Do you remember Gregory Barrett?"

"Oh, yes. I was genuinely sad to see him go. I couldn't say that of many of the others."

"He came to see me recently."

"What has he been doing with himself?"

"Teaching at Loyola, for one thing."

Hennessy groaned. "And what does he say when he runs into people who knew him as a priest?" The old bishop had another analogy. Spouses who divorced had once avoided the friends they had made in their married days. What were laypeople to make of a priest who got out of the priesthood? "It must make marriage seem equally escapable when things get tough."

"He also has a radio program, discussions of books. It's quite good. He developed it when he was living downstate, and its success led to the invitation that he broadcast it from Chicago."

"What does it matter where he does the program?"

"A program from Chicago has a greater chance of being picked up elsewhere. But there's more. A woman has accused him of improper conduct while he was a priest."

"Was a priest? *Tu es sacerdos in aeternum.*"

"When he was in the active priesthood. She claims he took advantage of her when she went to him for counsel."

"Dear God. Have you ever read Rabelais?"

"No."

"Don't. Very gamy stuff, and Rabelais himself was a priest."

"The woman got in touch with the archdiocese as they were ready to buy her off, but she refused."

"What does she want?"

"That's unclear."

"Does she think he will marry her?"

"Barrett already has a wife. And a son."

"I do remember Barrett, Roger. I can't believe he would have been mixed up in such a thing."

"Should I suggest to him that he come see you?"

Hennessy thought about it. "Does he smoke?"

Roger rose to go, and the bishop asked for his blessing. He gave it, and received the bishop's in his turn.

"What I could never understand in those who left, Roger, was how they could face a future in which they would no longer say Mass."

❧ Part Two ❧

Against his inclinations and against his habit, Captain Philip Keegan had taken a vacation this year. Oh, he always took several weeks, usually in the winter, but he did not leave Fox River, just tried to be lazy, sleeping late, sometimes until nine in the morning, if he had sat up late watching television and drinking beer the night before. And he would spend more time with Father Dowling. All along he was sustained by the thought that he was easily within reach if anything important came up. Just to make sure, he would call Cy Horvath once a day to hear how things were going in his absence. But this year had been different.

For years, his married daughters had pleaded in vain for him to visit. He resisted because they lived on opposite ends of the country, and visiting neither could be presented as evenhandedness. Now, though, his granddaughter Nell, named for her grandmother, was to make her first communion in Charleston. Cecilia, his daughter, insisted that he must come.

"And don't say you're afraid of hurting Norah's feelings. She and Oliver and little Jimmy will be here, too. Dad, it will be a family reunion."

It was an invitation he could not refuse, and so he accepted. A family reunion. He had been alone now for seven years, but he still dreamt of his wife and sometimes came awake at the call of her voice. In the wee hours of the morning, the hard-nosed captain of the Fox River police sometimes wept himself back to sleep.

So he had gone to Charleston, and there had been a family reunion with both his daughters and their families. He even got along fairly well with his sons-in-law, though one was a Democrat and the other something worse, a pacifist and against the death penalty besides.

"Of course, it's simply the Catholic position now," Oliver said smugly.

"I hadn't heard."

His son-in-law Ronald asked if he didn't still see a lot of his priest friend Roger Dowling. He said he did, hoping it would change the subject.

"Ask him," Oliver said. "He'll tell you."

Keegan let it go. His daughters loved their husbands, and that was good enough for him.

Little Nell looked like an angel in her white dress and veil, her hands clasped over her brand-new prayer book. If only her grandmother could see her.

"I'm sure she does," said Norah, and Cecilia agreed. He hugged and kissed them both.

From Charleston, he went on to Sarasota and the condo on Siesta Key he had rented for two weeks. Two weeks. It seemed a sentence he must serve. Oliver thought life imprisonment was the answer to capital punishment, but then his certitudes were grounded firmly in inexperience. Phil telephoned Roger Dowling from Florida and reported on the first communion.

"Get lots of sun, Phil."

"Sure. Roger, someone tried to tell me that a Catholic can't be in favor of capital punishment."

"I've heard the same thing."

"Is it true?"

"Why don't we talk about it when you get back? I don't want to run up your phone bill."

"I'd rather be hung myself."

"Than run up your phone bill?"

"Than spend the rest of my life in prison."

"Are you under arrest?"

"I'll be home in two weeks."

"Marie misses you."

"Haven't you fired her yet?"

A pause. "Then you heard?"

"Heard what?"

"Nothing, nothing. It can wait until you get home."

He couldn't get any more out of Roger. After the call, he walked along the shore with the waves endlessly rolling in, the water spangled with sunlight, the beach full of vacationers in various states of undress offering themselves to the sun.

When he got back to his condo, he called Cy Horvath, who said he didn't have any idea what Roger Dowling was talking about. It sounded like a lie.

There were places he could buy the Chicago papers, but asking for the *Fox River Tribune* was pointless. Finally, timing his call when Roger would be saying the noon Mass, he got hold of Marie Murkin.

"So you're still there?" he asked.

"Where else would I be? You forgot there's a time difference. Father is saying Mass."

"I talked to him a few days ago. I got the impression something was going on."

"Of course something is going on. We can't all run away to Florida and sit in the sun."

"That's good to hear."

"Well, thanks a lot."

He tried to let that call erase the effects of the previous one. If something was amiss, he could count on Cy and Marie and Roger to let him know. He went out on a charter fishing boat and, with help from Captain Jack, brought in a fair-sized marlin. He felt like an idiot being photographed with the thing. Then he had it dressed, frozen, and sent to Marie Murkin.

The trouble with doing nothing is that you get used to it. These were days when there was absolutely nothing he had to do, but still he developed a kind of schedule and kept to it. One night he got nearly drunk and decided to lay off drinking until he got home. Each day he x-ed out the date on the calendar. He got to the Sarasota airport three hours before his plane was due to leave.

He had the cab from O'Hare take him straight to his office— not the smartest idea, because showing up with the tan he had acquired invited comment. His secretary had made three piles on his desk, the third pile personal, so he got to that last. That was the first he knew of the article on Roger Dowling that had appeared in the Fox River paper. He winced as he read the piece. It had Marie Murkin's fingerprints all over it.

Cy came in while he was reading. "I heard you were back."

"Did you read this, Cy?"

His Hungarian lieutenant nodded. "That's what we're working on."

"What do you mean?"

"The man who wrote that? Ned Bunting. He's dead. Fished out of the Fox River early this morning."

On the western bank of the Fox River, there is a parking area to which young lovers repair, and some not so young. It was here that Pasquali had driven Gloria a week ago, turning in with a nervous laugh.

"Lovers' lane," he said.

"Is that the fast track?"

"I've never been here before."

"That's funny, I thought I recognized you."

Their friendship had waxed as hers with Ned Bunting waned, spurred by Pasquali's one-eighty on the quality of Gloria's paintings. They had been moved out of the staff lunchroom and were once more distributed about the reading areas and public places of the Benjamin Harrison branch of the Fox River library.

"They take getting used to."

"So did Picasso's."

"Tell me about your painting."

"Are you sure you don't want to see my etchings?"

Pasquali was of the type known in pop psychology as anal—that is, tight assed—and Gloria found this conducive to facetiousness. He seemed not to know what to do in reaction to her provocative remarks, but it was clear he loved them. His nervous laugh said it all.

"Tell me about Mrs. Pasquali."

"She is no more."

"Aww."

"One day I came home and found a note telling me she had gone. I read it over and over. I wept. And then I realized that she had done what one or the other of us should have done years ago."

"How many years?"

"Enough."

She had noticed that with her he kept his shoulders back and pulled in his midsection, the better to conceal his pot. Short curly hair formed around a tonsure on his pate.

"Tonsure?" he said. "I'm no monk."

"What's your sign?"

"Go?"

"Let's try amber for a while." But her arm pressed against his in the front seat of his Toyota. It had a glass roof that slid back, and she asked him to open it. Nice. Above them, weeping willows moved in the wind. "That must be nice at night."

"It's not so bad right now."

He was allegedly at a meeting in the Loop. Gloria had told Ned that she was going on a one-day retreat. It was her third date with Pasquali, if that was the right word for it, and counting the time when she had disarmed him by making a gift of her paintings. When Maddie went back to her post, Gloria had sat on with Pasquali in his office. He seemed to be seeing her for the first time. For the matter of that, she had never really noticed him before, either.

The next day, he telephoned to express the library's thanks for her generous gift. "Of course, I have written a letter to that effect. You can claim it as a donation on your income tax."

"That will help."

"I could hand deliver it."

"On foot?"

She liked his nervous laugh. Some primal prudence suggested that she not have him come to the house. Ned had a bad habit of just dropping by. It occurred to her that the hapless writer was taking her for granted. Besides, she was a little tired of his lofty ambitions. The book he had given her to read was unreadable. When she told Maddie about it, she learned that Ned was not the author.

"Harry Austin just pours out fiction, all pretty much alike, all pretty bad. But people like it."

Gloria filed the information away under the heading "potential ammunition." And she thought Maddie was right to want to put an end to the crusade about her treatment by Gregory Barrett.

"What if I'm wrong, Gloria?"

"Then you'll be sorry you didn't take the money when it was offered."

"Would you have?"

"In a heartbeat."

So she said to Pasquali, "Why don't we meet at the Wahoo?"

"What's that?"

"A bar."

"I'm AA."

"It sounds like a battery. How about Bridgeman's?"

So they sat over ice cream like a couple of teenagers, her knee shoved against his. He didn't drink, but he smoked, so it wasn't all bad.

He said, "I haven't gone with anyone since Estelle left."

"Estelle."

"My wife."

"Maybe she'll come back."

"I divorced her. In absentia. For absentia." He had made a joke. Maybe it was contagious.

"Maybe you ought to."

"What?"

"Go with someone."

"Is that an offer?"

"We'll see. But I can't call you Louis."

"Why should you? My name's Fred."

"Mine's Daley." They shook hands.

When he drove her back to her place, Ned's car was parked at the curb. She was going to tell Fred to keep going, but what the hell, this could be fun.

"Come on and meet my usher."

Ned was half a head taller than Pasquali when they stood facing one another.

"Ned, this is Fred. The librarian."

"Did you have an overdue book?"

"No. I had a hot fudge sundae, and he had a banana split."

"I've been waiting here a half hour."

"Let's all go inside."

"Maybe Fred has an appointment," Ned said angrily.

"He does. With me." She put her arm through Fred's and sauntered to the door. Ned didn't follow. When she turned in the doorway, he was standing beside his car. He shook his fist at her.

"That man frightens me," she said as she let them in. "Now for my etchings."

She showed him her studio, and he stood openmouthed at the sight of so many paintings.

"Do you ever do anything else?"

"Only when asked."

He was uneasy in the confines of her house, she realized, and she found she wanted to play him like a fish. A fish she could learn to like.

"What are you doing tomorrow?"

"I have a meeting in Chicago in the afternoon."

"We'll have lunch first."

She went to the door with him and saw that Ned was still out there, standing by his car. Gloria watched as Fred marched out to his. Ned advanced on him, mad as a wet hen, or rooster. Fred just looked at him calmly. Ned put a hand on his arm and then, in a trice, Fred had taken it, twisted it, turned, and slammed Ned to the ground. He then went to his car, got in, and drove away. Gloria locked the door and went to a window. Ned managed to get to his feet, looked furtively at the house, then slunk to his car. After he drove away, Gloria heard music. She was singing, "They try to tell us we're too young."

The next day she and Fred had lunch, after which they drove to lovers' lane. "It's not that important a meeting."

While Gloria was looking up at the weeping willows, she felt his arm go around her shoulders.

"Why don't we walk?" she suggested.

They got out and walked. Paths led from the parking area to the river, and they took one of them. Fred was throwing stones in the water when Gloria noticed the body. She screamed. She backed away from the water, filled with dread. Fred went tentatively toward the body. Then he was running toward her. He took her by the arm and propelled her up the path.

"Was he . . ."

"Yes."

In the car, he got out his cell phone and punched at it. "Nine-one-one? There is a body in the river on the west bank." He hung up. "We don't want to be involved."

"No!"

"Did you see who it was?" he asked as he started the car. She looked at him with horror. "Your friend. The tall fellow. Ned Bunting."

Suicide? Ned Bunting's car was found illegally parked along the river road, as if he had stopped, crossed the road, and thrown himself into the river. The body had traveled some distance from the presumed spot from which he had jumped, but the reconstruction seemed obvious. In the trunk of the car were a portable computer and a tape recorder. They were impounded with the car. In the backseat were several writers' magazines, seemingly flung there.

"He just stopped to jump in the river?"

The medical examiner turned to look at Cy Horvath. "All this is just guesswork, of course."

But Cy's phlegmatic remark brought the guessing game to a close.

It was the plea of Gloria Daley, self-described particular friend of the deceased, that had initiated the search for Bunting.

"How particular?" Cy had asked her.

"We had become quite intimate. We were drawn together by our art."

Having turned the body over to Lubins, the coroner, and hoping that Lubins would wait and leave things in the capable hands of his assistant, Dr. Pippen, Cy had gone out to interview Ned Bunting's particular friend. They sat in a room every wall of which was covered with paintings.

"He painted, too?"

"He was a writer! He wrote that marvelous piece on Father Dowling, the pastor of St. Hilary's. It made quite a splash."

The remark seemed to refer to Bunting's entry into the Fox River, and Gloria Daley, who had been blowsy and flirty to this point, now decided to weep for her departed particular friend. "I can't believe he's gone."

Cy said, "Anything you can tell us will be helpful, Mrs. Daley."

"Oh, call me Gloria. I was never Mrs. Daley anyway. I took my own name back after I lost my husband." She rubbed her nose with a wadded Kleenex. "In Iraq."

They observed a moment of silence.

"So what can you tell us?"

She had first seen Bunting as an usher at the ten o'clock Mass at St. Bavo's, tall, imperious, never meeting any of the eyes he seemed certain were fixed on him. "When the priest came out and the Mass began, it was like a second act."

Cy had never seen an usher he hadn't wanted to kick in the rear, and the description of Bunting suggested he was the worst sort. "I'll check at St. Bavo's."

"Oh, he stopped going there. Monsignor Sledz insulted him, and we began attending Mass at St. Hilary's. That was another thing that drew us together, our faith."

"Insulted him?"

"Ned was a writer. Just before he settled on his new book project, he made an offer to Monsignor Sledz. He would do a short piece for the parish bulletin each week. Gratis. Sledz ridiculed the idea. He didn't just turn it down, he made fun of it. It is a tribute to Ned that such treatment did not shake his faith. Many people mistreated by the clergy never go to church again."

"Why the story on Father Dowling?"

"I needn't tell you about the priest scandal."

"Tell me everything, Gloria."

"Well, we were talking, Ned and I, about a book he might write, and just like that, the idea came. The priest scandal. The media have been playing it for all it's worth, but hostilely, as if every priest in the world is some kind of monster. Nonsense. So Ned decided that he would write on it from a local perspective, the Chicago scene, the archdiocese, that is, including all the suburbs, to show how small a thing it really is. That's why he decided to begin with the story on Father Dowling."

"It sounds as if he had a real goal there."

"Lieutenant, he was a man on a mission."

"So why would he commit suicide?"

"Suicide! Ned Bunting would no more commit suicide than I would." She almost glared at him. "We are Catholics."

No point in mentioning that from time to time a Catholic committed suicide. Not that it was certain that was how Ned Bunting had met his death.

"Well, if it isn't suicide, we are going to need an explanation. Like, who would want Ned Bunting dead."

Her eyes narrowed. "Does the name Gregory Barrett mean anything to you?"

"No."

"He's a regular on NPR."

"What's that?"

"National Public Radio!" She settled down and inhaled. "I will say no more. But you asked what I thought. NPR and Gregory Barrett. I will say no more."

Cy stood. "Did he like baseball?"

"Ned? Doesn't everyone?"

"Did he ever show you his bat?"

Her eyes glistened, but before she could say it he was out of the door. God, what a flake.

A Louisville Slugger had been found flung into the woods not far from where Ned Bunting's body was found.

"To think he sat at my kitchen table eating pineapple upside-down cake." Marie Murkin was on the phone to her counterpart Barbara at St. Bavo's.

"Monsignor Sledz thinks he should be buried from here."

"Well, he wasn't registered here, Barbara."

"Gloria Daley told the pastor that after the way he had treated Ned Bunting, driving him from the parish, it did not seem right to have his final send-off at St. Bavo's."

"Why should you care what she thinks?"

"Marie, there's no one else. No relatives, no close friends. No wonder he was susceptible."

"Susceptible?"

"To Gloria Daley."

"Ah."

"You don't think . . ."

"Let us leave that to the police," Marie said. "Anyway, could she have thrown him into the river?"

"Maybe he jumped."

"Barbara!"

Phil Keegan came by that night to watch a Bulls game with Father Dowling. Once the Bulls had been a bright spot in area sports, but with the departure of Michael Jordan things would never be the same again.

"So what about Ned Bunting?" Marie asked, holding Captain Keegan's bottle of beer until he had unwrapped his cigar.

"Death by drowning."

"I knew that much."

"Did you? Usually bodies pitched into the Fox River are already dead."

"He was pitched in?"

"Can't say. From what Cy has been learning, he was a troubled man. He thought he was a writer, but apparently no one else did."

"He was an usher at St. Bavo's."

"You think that was his motivation." He took the beer. Father Dowling was following this while he filled his pipe. A steaming mug of coffee was on the desk before him.

"He was more or less fired. He had been coming to Mass here," Marie said.

"And gathering material on the pastor," Father Dowling said from a cloud of smoke.

"I said I was sorry."

"How do you think I feel?"

"Did you ever meet the man, Roger?"

"Oh, Marie kept him all to herself."

"You think maybe he was a victim of a broken heart?"

Marie left them alone, her only comment something of a snort.

In the kitchen she wondered if she should have told Phil Keegan of the woman who had accompanied Ned Bunting to Mass. She made tea for herself and had the last of the pineapple upside-down cake, but it was dry and had lost its savor. She might have been punishing the two men, but Father Dowling never snacked, and Phil Keegan would not want cake with his beer.

She took from a drawer the issue of the *Tribune* that contained the story on Father Dowling, and read it as if it were a message from beyond. Anyone but Father Dowling would have been glad to have such a story written about him. If he had even read it. He was bothered as much by the accompanying photographs as by the story itself.

Marie was Irish enough to enjoy conjuring up the figure of the author. She looked at the chair in which he had sat and tried to remember the pleasant talk they had had here. Such a nice man, not at all awkward because of his height, and how deferential he had been to her. He had confided in her his intention of writing about these terrible stories about bad priests that had caused such a sensation. It was to counterbalance that that he had wanted to write about Father Dowling. Maybe she wasn't as sorry as she pretended. She pored over the story, trying to find traces of what she had told Ned Bunting.

Then her mind dwelled on the scandal of those stories. Say they were all true—and of course she knew that the clergy, too, were beset by the effects of original sin. Even so, it had been a good idea to give an account of a priest like Father Dowling and a parish like St. Hilary's. Her thoughts went to the visit Gregory Barrett had paid the rectory.

It had been a shock to learn that he was a priest; she couldn't say "former priest." Despite herself, she remembered her first impression of the man: highly favorable, no doubt about that. Then to learn that he was a classmate of Roger Dowling's who had gone off and married and had a child. She sipped her tea, and her eyes filled with tears at the thought of a man doing such a thing. He hadn't been the only one, far from it, but Marie's judgment of laicization was pretty much what it was of annulments. Still, it might be better to get permission to leave and marry and all the rest rather than remain in the priesthood and act the way some had. Wouldn't it have been better if all those bad apples had taken themselves out of the barrel? Not that that had spared Gregory Barrett from being accused of misbehavior.

"I don't believe it," Marie had told Father Dowling.

"No more do I."

Amos Cadbury would not have become the man's lawyer if he had thought him guilty, Marie was sure of that. How lucky she had been when Father Dowling had been appointed pastor. Marie had served as housekeeper for several years when the Franciscans had the parish. Little as she had thought of the friars, she was certain none of them had ever done anything he shouldn't have, but they had been a disorganized bunch, difficult to work for, and of course they had treated her like a housekeeper. With Father Dowling, Marie felt part of things, always told what was going on, when that was appropriate. Her eyes fell again to the newspaper story. No, she really wasn't sorry she had talked with Ned Bunting and told him what she had so that he could write so nicely of the parish. His allusions to Mrs. Murkin in the story gave some indication of how important she was to the smooth running of St. Hilary's. So she finished the cake and sipped her tea and mourned the loss of Ned Bunting.

Peanuts wasn't interested in the death of Ned Bunting, so Tuttle had gone downtown and hung around the pressroom to hear what he might hear.

Tetzel of the *Tribune* growled when the dead man was referred to as his colleague. "Quirk must have been drunk when he accepted that piece."

"Jealousy does not become you," Tuttle said.

"Jealousy!"

"He scooped you, Tetzel. And it was a great idea. Too bad you didn't think of it yourself."

"A puff piece. What kind of news is that?"

"It was his opening salvo, I'm told. He was going to do a book on the local angle of these scandals."

"A book!" Tetzel was alleged to have notes for a novel filed away on the hard drive of his computer.

"What was the public's reaction?"

"Check the letters to the editor. They loved it. Maybe we should run stories on people who haven't beaten their wives."

The others professed to be delighted by the suggestion, and Tetzel went back to his computer.

Tuttle pushed the Styrofoam cup of coffee from him. It tasted like last week. "Ciao," he said as he left the room.

"Peanuts teaching you Italian?" The words followed him out the door.

Upstairs he found Cy Horvath in his office talking with the black officer Agnes Lamb. He was used to the kind of look they gave him.

"I'm here to inquire about a client."

"A client."

"Mr. Ned Bunting."

Agnes reacted. "Haven't you heard?"

"Fill me in."

"How do I know he was your client?" Horvath reasonably asked.

"It was just a handshake, but with me that is sacred."

"Well, you're short a client, Tuttle. He was fished out of the Fox River."

Feigning surprise, Tuttle staggered to a chair, and Agnes sprang to her feet to help him get seated. She brought him a glass of water, which was welcome. It got the taste of the pressroom coffee out of his mouth.

"I suppose the reason for that handshake comes under privilege," Horvath said.

"He's dead?"

"Dead."

"Then all bets are off. He was writing a book on the clerical scandals. Local. You may have seen the marvelous feature he did on Roger Dowling."

"You need a lawyer to write a book?"

"There were those who did not sympathize with his project."

"Like Quirk."

"Quirk is an idiot. That piece on Dowling made news, yet he persisted in maligning my client."

"You think Quirk dumped him in the river?"

"Dear God. Is that what happened?"

In Tuttle's experience it was always wise to seek and not give information. He felt a momentary resentment at Peanuts's refusal to fill him in on Bunting. Then the manner of Bunting's death sent a tremor of fear through him—but what would the Pianone family have against Ned Bunting?

Agnes gave him a laundered version of the finding of the body and its transfer to the Fox River morgue.

"I would like to see his effects," Tuttle said.

Thank God for Agnes Lamb. She seemed to regard Tuttle as the next of kin. "Come with me." In the doorway she turned to Cy Horvath. Who could read that Hungarian face? But Cy nodded.

There were two baskets, one filled with what had been found on the body, the other with what had been found in Bunting's parked car. There was also a sheet of plastic and a baseball bat, the murder weapon. Tuttle recognized the tape recorder that Bunting had worn slung from his shoulder as if to announce WRITER AT WORK.

"Has anyone listened to that?"

Sportello, the custodian of the effects, lifted his shoulders in a gesture that could have meant anything.

Tuttle turned to Agnes Lamb. "Maybe you should be with me when I see what he had been taping."

Agnes Lamb signed out the tape recorder and led Tuttle to a

room where he could plug it in. "Go ahead," she said. "Just return it to Sportello when you're done."

"Bless you, my dear."

"Amen." She closed the door when she left.

Tuttle was electronically handicapped, and it took him some time before he mastered the mechanics of Bunting's machine. He huddled over it, listening to an exchange between Bunting and a woman, the subject Father Dowling. Ah, Marie Murkin. He fast-forwarded and soon was listening to the draft of the piece Bunting had done for the *Tribune*. More fast-forwarding and then silence. That was when Bunting noted the other tapes stashed in the pockets of the case that held the recorder. He had them in his own pocket before he had decided to take them. He sat for a while, pondering what he had done. There seemed little reason to fear any reprisals. Sportello was a zero, waiting out the time until he could retire and go on doing nothing in another venue.

Tuttle rewound the tape that was in the machine and listened again to the clearly delighted Marie Murkin feeding details of the life of Roger Dowling to Ned Bunting. Bunting spoke with the authority of an author, and Marie was clearly impressed. Tuttle listened for several minutes, then rewound the tape and took everything back to Sportello.

"Guard that with your life," he advised the lazy-lidded custodian.

"What is it?"

"It could be the smoking gun."

Sportello was still considering this remark as Tuttle sauntered down the hall, where he looked into Cy's office.

"Thank you, Officer."

Agnes gave a little bow. "Was it any help?"

"Not as much as I had hoped."

What would Peanuts say if he knew that Tuttle was thick as thieves with Peanuts's sworn enemy? Agnes Lamb had been hired as a gesture toward deflecting feminist and racist charges against the department, but she had soon proved herself to be an excellent cop, much to Peanuts's chagrin. There had been a time when the two of them rode in the same squad car, but within days Agnes was driving and Peanuts sulking in the passenger seat. Then Cy Horvath ordered her off patrol and under his wing, as solid an endorsement as any cop could get. Peanuts regarded it all as a conspiracy. In fact, it was his own presence on the force that was the conspiracy, an olive branch to the Pianone family. Otherwise unemployable, Peanuts drew his pay and was generally kept out of any matter of importance. The way he complained, you would have thought he wanted to earn his money, but his connatural racism and chauvinism explained his reaction to the rise of Agnes Lamb. Still, paragon that she was thought to be, she had made a large mistake in leaving Tuttle alone with the basket of evidence. He should have asked to see the personal effects as well. Maybe another time.

Back in his office, Tuttle asked Hazel if she had something he could play tapes on.

"Tapes."

"Cassettes."

"Music?"

"I think voice."

"I could play them on this." She pointed to the dictating machine on her desk.

"That's good to know."

"You want to play them or not?"

"Any calls?"

"Go to hell."

He went into his office, sailed his tweed hat at the coat stand, made a ringer, locked his door, and sat down carefully in his desk chair. The chair had a mind of its own and was likely to move at the slightest provocation.

There might be nothing on the two cassettes he had lifted from Bunting's case. They might even be blanks. No need to open himself to Hazel's criticism if he asked her to play the tapes and there was nothing on them. He would wait until she was gone and then see what he had.

A tap on the door. "You want coffee?"

"If it's made."

The door rattled. Tuttle pushed back and his chair carried him to the wall, hit with a bang, and dumped him on the floor. "I'm coming."

Hazel was framed in the doorway when he opened it. Her massive bosom was supported on her folded arms. "What do you do in there with the door locked?"

"Meditate."

"The imbecile called. He didn't leave a message. In fact, he didn't say anything. I recognized the breathing. It's like an obscene phone call."

"Peanuts?"

"How many imbeciles do you know?"

"Don't get me started."

"Come and have your coffee out here." She simpered. "I get lonesome."

She moved back toward her desk, where the coffee awaited, and he followed like a trained animal. He had no real defense against Hazel. Sometimes he thought she was older than himself, sometimes younger.

She had a bad habit of talking about how wonderful it had been with her first husband. "God, what a man he was."

"How many were there?"

"How many what?"

"You said your first."

"First and last, Tuttle. First and last. They broke the mold."

"What happened to him?"

"Cancer. He was gone in a month. You don't know what it's like for a woman to be left alone."

Tuttle had an idea what it was like for a man to be alone with a woman who has been left alone. "You should marry again."

"And leave you?"

There are modalities of female laughter, and Hazel's registered somewhere around the adolescent giggle. Since she had the build of a lady wrestler, this was incongruous.

"Good coffee."

"I am thought to be an excellent cook."

"You do Chinese?"

"Are you kidding?"

"It's my favorite."

"Stamp out rodents, eat Chinese. Do you know what they put in that stuff?"

It was four o'clock. Hazel left at five. If he sat here with her for an hour she would end up having him in a half nelson.

"I have been down to headquarters to check the effects of Ned Bunting."

"He never came to the office."

"He already had a girl."

She tried to punch him in the ribs, but he got out of range. "Those his tapes you want to hear?"

He laughed. "You think the police would let me walk off with something like that?"

"No. Did you walk off with them?"

"Hazel, I don't have to remind you that everything said in this office is under strict confidentiality."

"Give them here. I'll put them on."

So it was that Tuttle heard Bunting's last tapes. The first was a lengthy memo to himself, in which he seemed to be giving himself a pep talk about the book he hoped to write. Several old foes were mentioned, naysayers who would have to eat their words. "Or rather mine," Ned Bunting's recorded voice said. He repeated the phrase, obviously liking it. "Item. The ineffable Universal Literary Agency, a scam into which I sank five hundred useless dollars. Item. The moronic editor Max Zubiri, raking in money under false pretenses, exacting a fee to insult me. And then the superpompous Gregory Barrett, who acts as if he owns the authors he talks about. Who is he to dismiss my efforts? Quirk. Well, at least he took the piece on Dowling."

"I'll make a transcript for you," Hazel said. "In case the police notice they're missing."

"You can do that?"

"Tuttle, you'd be surprised what I can do."

6

Because encountering Tuttle of Tuttle & Tuttle posed such delicate problems of conscience, Amos Cadbury kept those encounters to a minimum. Should the little lawyer loom on the horizon in the courthouse, skating across the great granite floor beneath the cupola, doubtless having descended the great spiral staircase that did not interfere with the ground-level view of the allegorical depiction of justice up among the painted clouds—should Tuttle surprise him there, a simple nod from Cadbury sufficed. If he intended to enter an elevator, he made certain that this was not Tuttle's intention as well. Needless to say, Tuttle did not come to Cadbury's office or, if he did, was told some white lie that sent him away. Was this uncharitable or, as Amos wanted to think, a laudable shunning for the sake of the profession? If Amos had been truly vindictive, he would have pressed for Tuttle's disbarment on the two occasions he chaired the committee looking into Tuttle's activities. The few disbarred lawyers Amos Cadbury knew filled him with compassion. Oh, he believed in punishment for misdeeds, and he did not think life imprisonment was too severe a penalty for certain crimes, but for a man to be cut off from the knowledge and skills he had acquired in order to earn his bread, ah, that must be a veritable hell. So he had been lenient in judging Tuttle, hoping that the threat of disbarment would prove a stimulus to reform.

Now, dressing formally on the evening of the Fox River bar's annual spring banquet, Amos stood before his dressing room mirror and remembered times when his late wife's arm had lain on the arm of this dinner jacket. By half closing his eyes, he could conjure her up at his side, a replica of a photograph in his den of the two of them formally attired, taken by the ship photographer on the cruise that had marked the fiftieth anniversary of their marriage. The cruise had been aboard a Holland America vessel bearing the same name, *Statendam,* as that on which they had sailed to Europe on their honeymoon. There was another photograph of them with the pope, his bride now veiled in black, when they had attended the private papal Mass with a handful of others who had powerful friends in Rome. Why with his heart so full did he now think of the redoubtable Tuttle?

The reason occurred to him as he was driven to the hotel where the banquet would take place—in the Loop, there being no hotel adequate for the purpose in Fox River. In St. Peter's Square one was constantly accosted by men selling postcards and trinkets, men who would not take no for an answer and trailed along until defeat was certain. They seemed the very model of Tuttle seeking legal business by whatever means was effective. The annual banquet of the bar was the supreme test, since it would never do to snub a fellow lawyer on that occasion. He only wished that Tuttle were selling postcards and rosaries so he could make a purchase and be done with it.

The hour before the banquet was devoted to milling about and drinking in a huge room adjacent to the one in which they would dine. Amos's firm had, of course, reserved a table, and once there he would be surrounded by congenial colleagues. The social hour, though, was a time of maximum vulnerability, the more so because now Tuttle would not be wearing his trademark Irish tweed hat, which would have been sufficient warning even across the crowded room.

"Amos." A hand touched his elbow, and he turned to see, almost with relief, that it was Barfield. The two men exchanged greetings, and Barfield, who now had a grip on Amos's elbow, led him off to relative privacy. "So you've seen Gregory Barrett."

Amos nodded.

"I had hoped that you would enlist his support in having that woman included in the arrangements the archdiocese is making for victims."

"Would persuasion work? In any case, he thinks it would be blackmail."

"Who's to say? But surely the aim must be to get such things behind us and out of the press."

"I can certainly say amen to that."

"His innocence in the matter is not to be taken for granted, you know."

"Proving that one has not done something is never an easy matter."

"You would let the charge go before a judge?"

Amos did not attribute the question to Barfield's well-known habit of bringing about mutually acceptable solutions without having recourse to a trial. Trials there must be; charges must be faced, a judgment awaited, that was the nature of the law—but in the case of wayward priests, the very accusation was a stigma on their whole order, and a swift resolution of the Barfield kind was a desideratum.

"That seems to be what Barrett wants," Amos said.

"He can be linked with the woman."

"Surely not in the way she charges."

"Do you know Tuttle, Amos?"

Amos winced.

"I know, I know. But the rascal has turned up records that you should know of before you proceed."

"What prompted him to seek such records?"

"That you must hear from him. I asked him to call on you tomorrow. You won't regret it." Off Barfield went, mission accomplished, squeezing elbows as he disappeared among the crowd.

If Tuttle was at the banquet, Amos did not see him. Several members of the firm were called up to receive awards and recognition. There was a shamelessly long talk by a politician, allegedly expert in legal matters. There were blessedly brief appearances by a rabbi, a monsignor, and a well-known evangelical preacher. Amos saw a number of dear old friends before calling for his car. On the drive home, the one memorable event of the night seemed to be Barfield's remark about Tuttle.

When he told his secretary, Miss Sullivan, that if Mr. Tuttle came by he would be in to him, she reacted as if he had announced that he would be meeting with a member of the Pianone family to deliver or receive a bribe.

"Mr. Barfield has sent him to me."

Like many legal secretaries, Miss Sullivan could doubtless pass the bar exams, argue a case in court, and do almost everything else a lawyer does except conceal her true estimate of people. Barfield was not one of her favorites, perhaps more because of the amount of publicity he managed to get than for the bargaining that had made him famous.

"Father Dowling called."

"Ah."

"Should I get him on the line?"

"Later." Into his office he went. Something told him that Tuttle would be here bright and early—well, say ten o'clock—and that he wanted to see the man before he talked with Father Dowling.

Tuttle arrived at 9:45 and was announced in frosty tones.

"Send Mr. Tuttle in."

Tweed hat in hand, Tuttle entered. He still wore a topcoat; his necktie was knotted several inches below his open collar. His smile was tentative.

"Barfield felt that I should bring you up to speed on what I have learned of the woman who has accused Gregory Barrett." All this before Tuttle sat on the edge of a chair, leaning toward Cadbury.

"May I ask why you are interested in the matter?"

"Mr. Cadbury, we share a client."

"Do we?"

"Gregory Barrett. He came to me after he had met with you and asked me to find out what I could about the woman accusing him."

Here was a situation in which Miss Sullivan would have failed. Indignation, anger, a sense of having been betrayed—these surged up in the Cadbury breast, but his expression did not change. "And you found something."

Tuttle took a crumpled sheaf of pages from his inner pocket, explaining that his secretary had typed up and printed out his notes. "Maybe I should just read this."

"Do."

Tuttle sat in the chair Gregory Barrett had occupied when he came to Amos with his problem. He had been persuasive in denying the charge against him. Now Tuttle, the ineffable Tuttle, while working on Barrett's behalf, had turned up what in the new cliché was called a smoking gun. Barrett had advised and counseled the woman when she was expecting a baby. He had made arrangements for her confinement. "It's all on the record, Mr. Cadbury." He had been further involved when the woman decided against giving her child up for adoption. All this could be explained in terms of pastoral care, but it was also susceptible of another and damning interpretation.

"Have you conveyed all this to Gregory Barrett?"

"Barfield advised me to talk with you."

"But Barrett is now your client."

"Oh, only for this."

"Detective work?"

"No detective could have found out what I have."

"You may be right."

"There is more. Ned Bunting, the man who wrote a piece on Father Dowling, was writing one on Barrett and the girl."

"The man who drowned?"

Tuttle decided against the tangent of talking about Bunting's death. He nodded.

"Had he found out what you have?"

"I wouldn't be surprised."

"Well, you have given me a great deal to think of. It was good of you to make these things known to me. What they portend, what I will now do, I cannot say, but I thank you for coming." Amos rose and extended his hand to Tuttle.

"What are friends for?"

It was not Tuttle that annoyed Amos now, but Gregory Barrett. Imagine going from this office to Tuttle! But would he himself have had someone look into those records? Perhaps Tuttle was the kind of lawyer needed in such a situation. Still, that could not excuse the duplicity of Gregory Barrett. Or had the man assumed that anything Tuttle turned up would be beneficial to him?

His parents' revelation of what they had been gave Thomas Barrett much food for thought. In the various Orthodox churches, priests have children and one might be the son of a priest without causing comment. The marriage had to be entered into prior to ordination, however, and a married priest could never become a bishop. On his father's shelf, Thomas Barrett had found a novel by Barbey d'Aurevilly called *Un prêtre marié* and tried to read it, but his shaky French did not permit it. Italian or German would have presented less problem: Tom's area of concentration was modern languages.

"The classics would make more sense," his father had said.

"English has become the lingua franca of the world, so how much use will modern languages have for you?"

"It's the literature I'm interested in."

Any opposition his father felt dissolved after that remark. If there was anything Thomas had absorbed from his upbringing, it was his father's bookishness. The move from Cairo had involved the transfer of the vast Barrett personal library and the building of shelves in almost every room of the new suburban house; mere furniture was a lesser problem. It was after they settled in Chicago that his parents had sat Thomas down and told him what he had vaguely suspected for years: His father was a priest and his mother was a nun.

There was an undeniably guilty note to the narrative. Both his mother and father expected him to see what they had done as needful of explanation.

"You have to understand what it was like, Tom. What I had been educated for, what I had looked forward to doing, was changing radically. A classmate of mine put it well. 'This is not the cruise I signed on for.' There was an exodus from the priesthood, and I was part of it. Your mother's case was even more compelling."

"My community decided to disperse, to live in apartments, to take jobs. What was the point of being a nun in such circumstances?"

Thomas found that he was trying to make it easy for them to tell him their story. If they had deserted their vocations, they had not lost the faith, and they had passed it on to him. He thought of all the Masses they had attended and wondered if his father ever thought that it could be him at the altar, vested, performing the altered but still ancient rite. When the great revelation was made, both his father and mother insisted that they had never regretted what they had done. Nor, of course, could he. His existence had followed from their decisions. They had known one another in their previous roles, they had discussed together what they intended to do, and they had done it together, and that formed a bond perhaps as binding as their marriage vows. Could they have repudiated those later promises as easily as they had the others? He doubted it.

"We have agonized over not telling you, Tom. But now that we are back in Chicago, you have to know."

What did they want from him—approval, censure, curiosity? He didn't know. Still, he was glad it was all in the open now. As for themselves, in Chicago they might at any time meet someone who had known them before, and that carried the threat that Tom would learn of their past in an accidental way. No, they were right to tell him, and he told them so.

Then there arose the question of his education. Would he continue in the school where he had a year to go? Already they had talked of where he would go to college. His parents favored Notre Dame. When his father was taken on at Loyola, it was decided that Tom would finish high school at Loyola Prep. A month after they made the move, they visited the campus at Notre Dame. After that, Tom's greatest fear was that he would not be admitted. Both his parents had visited the South Bend campus years ago. No need to say that it was when his father was a priest and his mother a nun. Not that they had been there at the same time.

There was no greater fan of *End Notes* than Thomas Barrett, not least because many of the programs developed from conversations he had had with his father. He was the only child they would ever have, and they doted on him, but not in a spoiling way. At least that was his judgment. His mother had been in her late thirties when she bore him and was warned against another pregnancy.

"You came into the world with a struggle," his mother said.

In the final semester of Loyola Prep, waiting to be accepted by Notre Dame for the following fall, the great blow fell. His father was accused of sexual misconduct during the years he was a priest. Discussing that was far more difficult than telling him of their previous lives. The chancery called, and the lawyer Barfield came to talk with his father. The woman had refused to become part of a group of victims the archdiocese was prepared to compensate for their traumatic experiences.

"What does she want?" his father asked.

"Do you have any memory of her?"

"As far as I know, I never met her." Barfield had brought a photograph, and his father studied it with puzzlement.

"Of course, that is a recent photograph," the lawyer said.

Barfield left it with his father, and Thomas later went into the study and looked into the photographed eyes of the woman who wanted to destroy his father. If it is possible to hate a stranger, Tom hated the woman. The mere accusation jeopardized the life his father had built during the years since he left the priesthood. NPR would not want to continue a program by a man considered guilty of taking advantage of a young woman while he was a priest. In the bio prepared by NPR, his father's education was recorded, but there was no spelling out of the fact that Mundelein was the major seminary of the Archdiocese of Chicago, graduates of which were ordained to the priesthood.

One Sunday they went to Mass at St. Hilary's in Fox River. His father wanted to get a sense of the classmate he had decided to consult about the problem he faced. He returned from his visit to the rectory encouraged, as if a cloud had been lifted. The further development of the charge against his father was discussed in whispers by his parents, and it was days before they could bring themselves to tell him that the woman was now ready to claim that Gregory Barrett was the father of her child. A son. It was clear to Tom that even his mother was shaken by this new charge.

"It's preposterous, of course. Tom, your mother is the only woman I have ever loved, and I mean in the full sense of the term."

So the cloud, a far darker cloud, returned. Tom believed his father, of course, but he could not keep himself from wondering if it were possible that he had a half brother. The resolution grew in him that he would find out who the woman was, find her, and get at least a glimpse of her son.

Amos Cadbury asked Father Dowling to dinner at the University Club and told him the new developments. It was clear that Amos was not amused that Barrett had enlisted Tuttle to find out what he could about the woman. What Tuttle had turned up looked devastating for Gregory Barrett. Father Dowling thought otherwise.

"Amos, a baby is a pretty definite thing. Whatever the charges have been until now, they are as nebulous as memory itself, but a child is real. I am assuming that he is still alive."

"Apparently."

"I don't know much about such things, but aren't there tests to determine parentage? I should think Gregory Barrett is in a far stronger position to determine his innocence now."

"Or guilt."

"Or guilt." Father Dowling sipped some water. It was seldom that he regretted that he no longer drank. Amos was having wine, a Sicilian red called Chaos, and it clearly enhanced his meal. In the club library previously he had had his customary manhattan. Later, again in the library, he would have some grappa. Anyone else could be expected to be *in medio jubilationis*, in the phrase, but Amos retained sobriety along with the mellowness alcohol confers.

"I met with Tuttle."

"You did?"

"Barfield sent him to me. In the circumstances I could scarcely refuse. Perhaps Barrett is right. Cases like this are street fights, and a battler like Tuttle is what is needed. I got the impression that Tuttle may be representing both sides in this dispute. Of course, I could not ask him that outright. He is such a scoundrel—but for all that I prefer him to some other legal colleagues. Ah, what the law has become, Father."

It was a familiar lamentation, but Father Dowling was more than willing to listen to his old friend's ruminations on what the legal profession had become during his long career. Change for Amos was what it had been for Aristotle, more the cause of decline than advance. Before they finished, Amos had got round to

Cicero, as he usually did. The great Roman advocate was a bit of a scoundrel himself and, in the days before transcriptions of trials, had written up his courtroom orations in deathless literary form after the fact.

"Who knows what relation they bore to what he actually said in court? In some cases, the written orations were never delivered in any form. Yet he had a certain nobility as well. He was ever conscious of living in a corrupt age."

"So he has become your patron."

"Oh, Thomas More is that." Amos sighed. "We Catholic lawyers have adopted him as our own, and what a judgment he is on us."

There is a kind of melancholy that is a consolation, and such was Amos's. He clearly derived strength from discovering parallels between his own situation and that of the two great men he had dwelt on.

"They were both executed for their principles. Who among us would stake his life on the position he argues? We have been taught that, because everyone deserves representation, the task of the lawyer is to take either side of a case and argue it as strongly as he can. The truth of the matter is supposed to emerge from the contest. Let us hope it does."

In the library, sipping his grappa while Father Dowling had another cup of coffee, Amos said, "I wrote a letter of recommendation for Barrett's son. He wants to go to Notre Dame."

"So he has been in touch."

"Not since I talked with Tuttle."

Although he had mentioned tests that could determine parentage, DNA having become the infallible mark of individuality if not of personality, Father Dowling found himself wishing that he could speak again with the woman. The thought returned the following day when Gregory Barrett came to the rectory of St. Hilary's.

Marie announced him with somewhat less unction than she had the first time he visited. It was clear from Barrett's manner that recent events were weighing on him, so he did not notice any alteration in Marie's reception. The two men settled in the study.

"I am afraid I have offended Amos Cadbury, Roger."

"By enlisting Tuttle's support?"

Barrett nodded. "And he did come through. But now I am accused of having fathered the woman's child."

"I have spoken with Amos."

"Tuttle did what Cadbury would never do, at least personally. I suppose there are lesser beings in the firm to whom he could have assigned such detective work. Roger, I did know that woman. I honestly had no memory of her when I came to you before, but what Tuttle has discovered has prodded my memory. And it is no longer simply a question of memory. She came to me in trouble. She had resisted the advice that she abort her child, and I made arrangements for her confinement."

"That is not a word one hears much anymore."

"It occurs frequently in Jane Austen." He sounded nostalgic for the eighteenth century. "All that is on record. I am on record as the one who smoothed her way. Of course, the idea was that she would give the child up for adoption, but she decided against that as well. How it all ended, I don't know, but I am sure now that I did what I am said to have done."

"Surely not fathered the child."

"Not that! As God is my judge, Roger, I was a virgin when I married Nancy."

"Then I would say that your position is far better than it was. There are tests to determine whether a man is the father of a child."

Barrett sat back. "Of course there are."

"So the whole matter can be resolved objectively. It will no longer be a matter of what you remember or of what she remembers."

"But will she agree?"

"It is the son who will have to agree."

"Of course."

"It remains a delicate matter, Greg. Whatever her motives, she has gotten herself into a difficult situation. To this point, she has willingly adopted the role of a woman who had a child out of wedlock. You and I and Jane Austen would take that as a negative mark, and yet she has publicly insisted on it. Accusing you has made her a bit of a heroine to others, perhaps to herself. But if it is established that her child is not yours, she will become an outcast woman even in these permissive times. I would like to speak to her again."

"Again?"

"She came to me."

Greg looked around him as if the study had become another place. "How could you possibly manage it?"

Would she want to see him again? "I have no idea, but I intend to try, and I think it well that you should know. No doubt the thought of confronting her has occurred to you as well. That would be threatening, far more so than if a poor fumbling pastor asked to have a few words with her."

Gregory Barrett left with a light step, and Father Dowling sat alone for half an hour, smoking his pipe meditatively. Of course

Barrett would think only of his own exoneration, but where would that leave the poor woman?

"Is he gone?" Marie asked, peeking around the door.

"You sound like one of the Bennet girls, asking about Mr. Collins."

Marie stared at him.

"Jane Austen."

"You're alone too much."

Hazel was somewhat mollified when Tuttle told her to send a bill to Gregory Barrett, for services rendered. "He'll understand."

"I don't."

"Hazel, yours is not to wonder why—"

He got into his office and out of range of the ballpoint she threw at him. Who was that saint whose body was filled with darts? Hazel should know that any object, however seemingly harmless, can become a weapon.

His heart was not in it. He sat behind his desk and settled his tweed hat over his eyes, intent on reviewing recent events. He had reason to feel a sense of accomplishment, but the feeling would not come. His phone rang; he tipped back his hat. Hazel on the intercom.

"Yes?"

"How about the son?"

"What about him?"

"Real lawyers charge for office visits."

"Let's wait on that."

Thomas Barrett had come to see him. He had found the lad chatting with Hazel in the outer office some days ago when he returned from lunch with Peanuts. Hazel was at her oily worst, all over the kid, half flirting, half maiden aunt. They were talking about Notre Dame. Thomas Barrett turned when Hazel cried out like the announcer of the Mr. America pageant, "Here he is!" Her eyes danced with significance. "This is Thomas Barrett, Mr. Tuttle."

Tuttle shook the lad's hand and looked him over. "Your father's my client."

"That's why I've come."

Hazel actually got up and opened Tuttle's door. The kid went in; Hazel gave him a locker-room slap on the bottom and then closed the door on lawyer and possible client.

"I wanted to tell you personally how grateful I am for what you have done for my father."

Here was a welcome note. Tuttle would cede to no man in the devotion he felt to his late father. Through thick and thin, the elder Tuttle had supported and encouraged the younger. The long years in law school, the many efforts to pass the bar, the opening of this office—how differently things might have gone with him but for that paternal support.

"Anyone could have found out what I did."

"But no one did. If you hadn't found those records, my father would never even have remembered that woman. Now the matter can be settled, once and for all."

Tuttle liked Thomas Barrett more by the minute. Here was filial piety of a kind now all too rare.

"I mean DNA."

Tuttle nodded. A Greek of the fourth century B.C. knew more science than did Tuttle in the third millennium.

"I've brought you a sample." He carefully took an envelope from his pocket. It contained several items. One was a cotton puff, slightly discolored. "Blood," the boy explained. "And here is his toothbrush." He put these treasures on Tuttle's desk. Then he took out another envelope. "I hope this will be enough." Another toothbrush. Tuttle looked at it, then at the boy. "Marvin's. Her son. I thought about going to some lab myself and having the tests run, but then thought it ought to be a third party. A professional person."

He meant Tuttle. The little lawyer looked at the items on his desk as a member of a cargo cult might have studied unintelligible artifacts washed ashore on his obscure island. Then the realization came. DNA. O.J. Of course. With these items, Tuttle could settle Madeline Murphy's accusations once and for all. And the boy was doing this for his father.

"You've done exactly the right thing. I've been wondering how I could get hold of such materials," Tuttle said.

"How soon can you do it?"

"How does now sound to you?" He rose, scooped up the items, and put them in his pocket. "What's this about Notre Dame?" he asked as they emerged into Hazel's office.

"I've been accepted for the fall."

"Some of my best friends have gone there." He avoided Hazel's eye. "Amos Cadbury, for one."

"Have you got your cell phone with you, Mr. Tuttle?" Hazel asked.

He patted his pocket. He would have liked to prolong the scene, if only to have Hazel address him as Mr. Tuttle a few more times, but delay was out of the question.

"I prefer walking," Tuttle said, as they passed the useless elevator and headed for the stairway.

"I walked up. I got tired of waiting for the elevator."

"A busy place," Tuttle said. "A busy place."

They parted outside the building, but not before Tuttle thought to ask Thomas Barrett if he had told Hazel the purpose of his visit.

"Oh, no."

"Good. Not that the information would not be safe with her. A lawyer needs a secretary he can trust."

They shook hands again, and again Tuttle thought, *What a splendid boy, what a good son.* He drove off to police headquarters, parked in a place reserved for reporters, and went up to Cy Horvath's office.

"What do you know about DNA, Cy?"

"They are three letters of the alphabet."

"Exactly. Let me tell you what I have. Can I close that door?"

"Are you leaving?"

Tuttle shut the door, returned to Cy's desk, and brought out the envelopes. He let Cy peek in. "This one has things of Gregory Barrett's. This one has the toothbrush of his alleged son. Can we talk to Pippen?"

Dr. Pippen, the assistant coroner, did all the actual work, Lubins being an ass, in office for purely political reasons. She was a woman in her midthirties, tall and willowy, with a head of golden blond hair gathered into a saucy ponytail. She plunged her hands into the pockets of her lab coat when Cy told Tuttle to tell the doctor what he had. "I suppose those things would be sufficient. It's not my bailiwick, you know."

"But you know someone who would know?"

"Oh, sure."

Tuttle listened with satisfaction to the instructions Cy gave Pippen. It would be handled as an official police matter. No need to identify A and B, whose effects were in the envelopes.

"Who are they, by the way?"

"Supposedly father and son," Tuttle said.

Pippen's green eyes sparkled. "I think I can guess."

"Don't," Cy said. "We want hard science, no guesses."

Now, seated at his own desk, Tuttle awaited the results of that test. He found that he was of two minds on the matter. Would every dispute eventually be settled by such impersonal testing as this? Where would that put the legal profession, with its traditional reliance on bad arguments, worse inferences, and resounding rhetoric? (Tuttle was remembering a sentence in a law journal that favored such testing and sought to make its case by denigrating lawyers.)

Hazel had asked if he should bill the son as well as the father, but Tuttle would settle for what he was sure would be the undying gratitude of the splendid young man.

* * *

Tuttle had fallen asleep under his tweed thinking hat, so deeply that he did not hear Hazel's buzz. She came in and shook him awake. Tuttle did not come gently into this kind day. He looked wildly at Hazel and pushed back from his desk, sending his chair spinning against the wall. When it struck, it dumped him unceremoniously onto the floor.

"You awake now?"

"Help me up."

She nearly jerked his arm from his socket when she pulled on it. The motion brought him into a standing position, pressed against her enormous breasts. He could both hear and feel her breathing. Terror gripped him, and he broke free.

"Lieutenant Horvath called," she said.

"Ah. And what's the verdict?"

"Verdict?"

So Tuttle told Hazel what Thomas Barrett had brought him.

"Jesus, Mary, and Joseph." Hazel blessed herself.

"Are you Catholic?"

"No, but I saw the movie."

Part Three

Cy reviewed the investigation into the death of Ned Bunting. A patrol car checked out the report and verified that it was authentic. Soon the parking area was filled with official vehicles: a fire truck, the paramedic ambulance, half a dozen patrol cars. Officers were keeping back the citizens who had followed the sirens to their destination. Cy got there about the same time Pippen did. People stepped back to let them through. The body had been taken from the water but left close to where it had been found when it was clear the man was dead.

"A tall drink of water," Pippen said.

"It looks like that's what he had."

"We'll see."

Cy loved to watch Pippen in her professional role. She had slipped on latex gloves and knelt by the body, doing this and that. She stood. "Let's take him in."

So the tall drink of water was poured into a rubber bag and carted up to the paramedics' vehicle, to be taken off to Pippen's morgue. Meanwhile, Cy was examining the cordoned-off area, maybe fifty square feet at the edge of the water. It looked to him as if the body had been dragged into the water. Along that path? The condition of the bushes and weeds suggested the way he had come to his watery grave. Cy pointed this out to the lab men and then got out of their way. In the woods, some ten yards from the area where the body was examined, he found an old sheet of plastic, four or five feet long, and a baseball bat. He instructed the crew to take those along as well.

Pippen was standing with folded arms in the parking area, watching the vehicle carrying the body being directed through the gathering crowd. "And I was just telling Lubins how slow things have been."

"That sounds like a motive."

"I better get back."

"Wanna race?"

"I'll see you there."

The identification of the body presented no problems. There was a wallet in his trousers with multiple ID: a driver's license, a card saying he was a lifetime subscriber to *Writer's World*, and some holy cards, apparently memorials of his parents.

"Edward Bunting," Pippen said into the microphone that dangled from the ceiling over her workplace. Cy was at the observation window. She began carefully to undress the body, failing to find anything of significance in the clothes. "He didn't drown."

Cy was preparing to go back to his office, not having the stomach for what he thought Pippen would do next. But she lifted the cadaver several times, her arms under the shoulders. "Broken neck," she said. Then one of her ghoulish instruments began to whirr, and Cy got out of there.

*   *   *

"Bunting?" Phil Keegan said.

"Edward Bunting."

Phil shook his head. "That must be the Ned Bunting who wrote the puff piece on Roger Dowling."

"He was found in the river, but Pippen says he didn't drown. His neck was broken. It was pretty obvious that he was dragged down to the water and thrown in. The lab will see what they can find."

Phil was already on the phone to Roger Dowling. "I can understand your resentment, Roger. It was a pretty bad article, but this is going too far."

There was a smile on Keegan's tanned face that gave some indication of what he had been like as a kid. He and Dowling were old friends, and the phone call was the equivalent of playground teasing.

Marie Murkin acted as if the death of Ned Bunting were divine retribution for her cooperation in the article on the pastor of St. Hilary's, and Father Dowling did not try to unravel her snarled theory. Meanwhile, over the next several days, he was kept apprized of the ongoing investigation.

The deceased was indeed the author of that memorable tribute to Father Dowling that had appeared in the *Tribune*. Phil Keegan settled into a chair in the study.

"He thought of himself as a writer, Roger. Quirk said he couldn't write his way out of a wet paper bag."

"Faint praise, Phil. So why did he print it?"

"He said it was an off day."

More people remembered Ned Bunting as an usher at St. Bavo's than as a writer. Apparently he'd had some sort of tiff with the pastor there.

"Monsignor Sledz," Roger said.

"Yes. Barbara Blaisdel, the housekeeper, said it had something to do with the parish bulletin. Bunting had offered to do a weekly column for it, and Sledz laughed him out of the rectory."

"He had been coming to Mass here."

"With a woman," Marie said from the hallway. She looked in and said to Phil Keegan, "Ask Barbara who she was."

"I thought you wanted to be a priest, not a detective."

Marie's eyes lifted to the ceiling, and her lips moved in prayer. Marie Murkin was the last of the male chauvinists when it came to the role of women in the church. How many of the apostles were women? This observation provided all the argument Marie was likely to make. How do you argue for the obvious?

"Thanks, Marie," Father Dowling said.

"You're welcome, I'm sure. I don't know about whatshisname there." She was gone.

"Bunting was with a woman when she came here, according to Marie."

"I'll talk to Barbara Blaisdel."

When Cy had talked to Gloria Daley, he learned that Bunting's great project was a book about the priest scandal.

Pippen's report on her examination confirmed that Bunting had not drowned but had died of a broken neck. Only then had he been put into the water.

"He was a big guy," Phil said. "Putting him in the river would have taken quite an effort."

The examination of the scene at the edge of the river confirmed Cy's guess that the body had been dragged through the underbrush to the water. There were several pretty obvious paths, but they had been avoided. The question was, where had the fatal injury been inflicted? The parking area was impossibly contaminated by all the official vehicles and then by the curious who had come to the scene of the discovery of the body of Ned Bunting.

Cy had been there when the lab crew went over Bunting's residence. It was a small bungalow in which he had been raised by his parents and where he had stayed on after their deaths. Two bedrooms, living room, dining room, kitchen. The place looked as it must have looked when Bunting was a boy, very old-fashioned but neat as a pin.

"The basement was the thing."

The furnace, hot water heater, and washer and dryer were housed at one end of the basement, in a room built especially to keep them from view. The rest of the area was covered by indoor/outdoor carpeting. A long table ran the width of the short wall, and on it were a massive computer, a printer, a fax machine, a telephone, and a television set hooked up to a video and CD player. The lighting over the work area was provided by fluorescent lights. The rest of the area was devoted to comfort. There were several bookshelves, a couch, an easy chair, and a large coffee table strewn with publications. A massive ashtray was within easy reach of the chair. It was here that Ned Bunting had nursed his ambition to be a writer. On the walls were portraits of his heroes: a bearded Hemingway, a forlorn Scott Fitzgerald, Philip Roth making the most of what hair he had, John Updike looking a bit like a rabbit.

"No sign of a struggle."

"Not in the physical sense." You never knew when Cy was being less than serious. The basement room would be subjected to close analysis, the results of which would take time.

Meanwhile there was the question of Ned Bunting's funeral, and that concerned Father Dowling more directly. Gloria Daley came to the rectory, spoke at length with Marie, and then was led in to the pastor.

"I think it would be wrong for Ned to be buried at St. Bavo's," she began, and told the story of the treatment to which Monsignor Sledz had subjected Bunting. "Now he claims him as an ideal parishioner, the best of ushers."

"Was he registered at St. Bavo's?"

"Father Dowling, we had been attending your Mass here. He had shaken the dust of St. Bavo's from his feet."

"Who are the next of kin?"

"I don't know anyone who was closer to him than I was."

"And she prefers here," Marie said.

"I'll talk to Monsignor Sledz."

Gloria was looking around the study. "If there was anyplace to hang it, I would give you one of my paintings."

Marie led her away.

Roger Dowling had no intention of getting into an argument with Sledz about the funeral of Ned Bunting. Sledz was a member of the Polish Mafia in the archdiocese and, like the rest of them, the salt of the earth. Imperious, of course, one who did not suffer fools gladly and who assumed that most of the laity were fools. It was easy to imagine his reaction to his usher's suggestion that he write a column for the parish bulletin, thus claiming parity with Sledz's weekly written address to his flock.

He telephoned Sledz and asked what he knew of the woman who had come to him with the request that Ned Bunting be buried from St. Hilary's.

"He was a parishioner here, Roger. Registered. He was an usher for years. We had a little misunderstanding and he got into a huff. He didn't try to register there, did he?"

"No."

"I should think that settles it, then."

"What undertaker will you use?"

"McDivitt."

"I suppose I could come and concelebrate."

Sledz hesitated. He probably thought of concelebrated Masses what Roger Dowling did. "One thing you might do, Roger, is lead the rosary at the wake tonight. The fact is, this is my poker night."

"McDivitt?"

"Seven thirty."

"I'll do it."

The death of Ned Bunting had made Tuttle reflective.

"It's almost like a death in the family," Tuttle said to Hazel, standing beside her desk in the outer office. "He was more than a client, he was a friend."

"I never met him." Thus do reports of disasters in far parts of the world inform us that no Americans were killed. Hazel was incapable of abstract emotions: She had to know someone in the flesh and blood to like or hate the person. Even so, she could sympathize with Tuttle's stunned response to the death of Ned Bunting.

The news had reached him a day after the discovery of the body, and he did indeed at first feel it as a personal affront. He and Bunting had worked together on the Gregory Barrett case. Tuttle would never forget the unstinting admiration with which Bunting had listened to Tuttle's discovery of Barrett's role in the birth of Madeline's baby.

"You know what this means, Tuttle." Tuttle preferred to be told. He smiled wisely. "He's the father, Tuttle! That's what it means."

There was no point in quarreling with this interpretation. For

Tuttle, it was easier to believe that then-Father Barrett had been what help he could to a young woman in distress. Bunting, though, was aflame with certainty. "Let's tell Gloria."

In the event, it was Bunting who had told Gloria, in the course of the narrative failing to mention that the great discovery had been made by Tuttle. No matter. There was something unsavory in Bunting's eagerness.

Gloria listened with concern. "What will Maddie say when she hears?"

"Let's find out."

"No." She laid a hand on Bunting's arm. "I'll talk with her first. Who knows what trauma this will cause?"

"We got him," Bunting had said, hugging himself. "We've got the smug sonofabitch."

Such triumphalism was unseemly, and Tuttle was happy to get away into the company of the phlegmatic Peanuts Pianone. Peanuts wanted Italian rather than Chinese for lunch.

"What is it, a holy day?"

"Every day is a holy day."

Well, every day was a holiday for Peanuts. Lunching with Peanuts was no obstacle to thought, and Tuttle had reviewed where he was at that time, professionally.

Gregory Barrett was no longer his client, so there was no conflict of interest in gathering information harmful to him. Bunting was a client. How about Madeline? The trouble with that was that she was unlikely to be dunnable for any significant amount no matter what happened. He might as well be acting pro bono. Bunting's reaction had brought home to Tuttle that he had little taste for this crusade against the clergy. Of course, the targets were bad apples, but not everyone who joined the pack was all that discriminating about the objects of pursuit.

Later, in the pressroom at the courthouse, Tetzel was holding forth on the scandals. "It all comes down to celibacy," he pontificated. "These guys are lonely."

"You ever been married, Tetzel?"

The reporter ignored the hostile question. "Take Tuttle, now. He's a celibate, sure, but that's his nature."

Tuttle took umbrage at this; he wasn't sure why. He had never thought of himself as a celibate before.

"So let priests get married?" someone asked.

"Sure. Why should they be happy?"

Tuttle left. Hours of idleness might be the explanation of the resentment reporters felt for the rest of the world. They brooded too much. The scramble for news was demeaning. No wonder they hated the politicians they had to grovel before.

And when Ned Bunting's body was found on the western shore of the Fox River, in lovers' lane, Tetzel, of course, had a theory. "Look, he talks some Amazon into parking with him, he gets fresh and gets his neck broken."

"A woman?"

Light suddenly gleamed in Tetzel's eyes. "You may be right. What do we know about Bunting's personal life?"

"He was an usher at St. Bavo's."

"A perfect cover. We'll check out the altar boys for complaints against him. I say it was a question of rough trade. When I was in the navy—"

He was drowned out by the groans of his fellow members of the Fourth Estate.

Upstairs, Tuttle walked into Cy Horvath's office and said, "What do we know?"

"Quite a lot."

Tuttle sat. "For instance."

"Well, two and two are four. The sun is ninety-three million miles away, the average lifetime of the fruit fly is—"

"I mean about Ned Bunting."

"I should be asking you, Tuttle. You were a friend of his."

"I knew him, yeah."

"Tell me about him."

Cy was serious, putting Tuttle in an unusual position. His visits to the offices on the top floor of the courthouse were made to gather, not give, information—but this was a special case.

"He was a writer."

"What had he written?"

"He had a story about Father Dowling in the *Tribune*."

"What else?"

"He was engaged on a project. He wanted to write a book on the priest scandal."

"Tuttle, people keep telling us the guy was a writer, but no one knows what he wrote except that thing on Dowling. Isn't a writer someone who writes?"

"Horvath, you have no soul. You don't understand artists, writers, painters."

"Painters?"

"Gloria Daley was a friend of Bunting's. She paints. Some of her things are on display at the Benjamin Harrison branch of the public library."

"A particular friend."

"Kindred spirits. She is also the friend of Madeline Murphy, the woman who accused Gregory Barrett."

"Hence the book idea?"

"You got it. What about those tests?"

"Pippen will let me know when she gets the result."

"They're pretty important, you know."

"Tuttle, why don't you find Peanuts and exchange great ideas?"

When the body was discovered, Nancy Barrett said to Gregory, "Have you heard? They found that fellow Ned Bunting in the river."

"Dead?"

She nodded. What could he say? The thought of Ned Bunting just disappearing from the face of the earth had been an attractive one for weeks. They had discussed the threat posed by the record that had been found—he, Nancy, and Thomas.

"What kind of a creep would scrounge around looking for that kind of stuff?" Thomas asked.

"The role of Torquemada is always attractive."

"Poetic justice," Thomas said now.

Afterward, it occurred to Gregory Barrett that none of them had expressed regret at the death of Bunting. Understandable, perhaps, but not very Christian. Then again, what kind of Christians were they, after all? He and Nancy had explained abandoning their vocations as the result of having been let down by the Church. It was as if what they had done were the principled, the noble thing. Well, it had been the right thing, he was sure of that. In the intervening years, the developments in the Church had seemed to justify what they had done. Of one thing he was certain: He could not have faced all those changes with equanimity. At Mass—and they went nearly every Sunday—he found himself dismayed by the liturgical changes. The priest, now called the presider, smiled out at the congregation, an emcee there to hold their interest and entertain them. Criticism came easily because it was a species of self-justification. He marveled at the way Roger Dowling had adjusted to all the turmoil. The day after Bunting was found, he went again to St. Hilary's, just dropping by.

"Father is saying the noon Mass." The housekeeper could scarcely disguise her disapproval of him.

"I'll go over to the church."

When he came in, an old fellow with a croaking voice was reading the scriptural passages of the day while Roger Dowling sat behind the altar. Of course, he read the gospel and followed it with a four-minute homily—Barrett timed it—a brief and pointed commentary on the story of the ten lepers. Roger suggested that the story could be read in two ways: only one of ten or at least one of ten. He exhorted them to be that tenth cleansed leper.

Roger said the Roman canon, which was the one they had grown up with. For a short time, Barrett could imagine that the old thing went on, that the changes were superficial. Roger's fidelity to his vocation seemed something to envy.

Barrett did not go forward at communion time. What was the condition of his soul? His soul had become a stranger to him, ceding its primacy to mind and his love of literature. In his next program, he would speak of Trollope and Lily Dale's reaction to being jilted by Crosbie. An impossibly, unbelievably good woman, worthy of Dickens. But he would contrast Lily with Mrs. Lupex and Amelia at John Eames's boardinghouse. Trollope could write truly about women, but he had a fatal weakness for females like Lily Dale. Even as he prepared the program, Barrett found himself congratulating himself on his perception. It all seemed trivial watching Roger Dowling say Mass.

Afterward, he went into the sacristy where Roger greeted him warmly. "Good. You must have lunch with me."

"Oh, I couldn't do that."

"And why not?"

"I don't think your housekeeper approves of me."

"Would you want her approval?"

"You certainly have it."

"You see? She has abysmally low standards."

When they took their places in the rectory dining room, Marie Murkin was on her best behavior, and Barrett relaxed.

"Do you know, when I visited you a few weeks ago, it was the first time I had been in a rectory since I left. Now here I am in the dining room."

"Where did you speak with Equivocal Casey?"

The meal was passed discussing Casey and other professors they had had. What fun it was. Afterward, they went to the study, where they could smoke.

"Have you heard about Ned Bunting?" Greg asked.

"Poor fellow. I commemorated him in today's Mass."

"I didn't hear that."

"No reason why you should have recognized it. I just referred to him as Edward."

"That was good of you."

"He had been coming to Mass here."

"Do you know how he died? The news reports are vague, but they suggest drowning."

"He died of a broken neck."

"Good Lord." Barrett drew on his cigarette. "You're sure?"

"I have friends in the police. Do you remember a fellow named Phil Keegan at Quigley? A class or two below us."

"No." He rubbed the tip of his nose with the back of his hand. "Not that my memory has been all that reliable."

Roger ignored that. "He left and went into the service, served as an MP, and became a policeman when he got out. He is now captain of detectives. We've become great friends."

"Do they have any idea who did it?"

"Not yet."

"You know what I fear, Roger."

"Tell me."

"I will seem to have had a pretty good motive for wanting to get rid of him."

"So would I, for that matter. Abstractly, I mean. My hagiographer. I can't tell you how I was teased about that ridiculous piece."

"Watching you say Mass, I don't think it was all that ridiculous."

"Well, I know where I was and what I was doing at the time he was apparently killed. You do the same, and we will both go unscathed."

"When exactly did it happen?"

"The body was found on Wednesday afternoon. It would have happened earlier that day or late Tuesday."

"I tape my broadcast on Wednesday morning."

"There you are."

"I haven't done anything about a DNA test. Of course, I would have to get something of her son's."

Roger was thoughtful for some moments. "Maybe that won't be needed now. With Bunting dead."

What caught Agnes Lamb's attention was the 911 call. She had it played over several times: an excited male voice, the blunt message, and then the connection was broken. If the call had been made from the place where the body was found, he must have used a cell phone. There were three local cell phone companies, and Agnes visited them all. The first one bristled at the request for a list of their local customers.

"You're right," Agnes said. "Until I get a court order, that is. In the meantime, why don't we check the calls made last Wednesday afternoon. Say about midafternoon."

Privacy is a lost concept in the information age. Everything is recorded somewhere—ATM transactions, credit card uses, cell phone calls. Neither of the first two companies recorded a midafternoon call to 911 on the previous Wednesday. The third service neither refused to let her see the list of their customers nor hesitated to check the calls. There it was, 3:15 P.M. Actually, there were half a dozen calls in the relevant period, but only one to 911.

"Whose number is that?"

The list of subscribers was printed out for her, and Agnes, feeling she had violated more than a penumbra of the Constitution, took it as if it were the most routine thing in the world.

"Check it out," Cy Horvath said when she reported to him.

Pasquali, Pasquali. Why did the name sound familiar? She went downtown and fooled around with the departmental computer, doing a search for Pasquali. There it was, in a complaint from a librarian at the Benjamin Harrison branch.

She pulled into a handicapped spot and went into the library, in uniform, complete with cuffs and pistol and a belt filled with mean-looking rounds. She felt as if she were entering a saloon in a western.

The woman behind the counter lit up at the sight of her. "Finally," she cried. "Look at them." She pointed at the bank of computers, all commandeered by shady-looking men staring at the monitors with popped eyes.

"Inquiring minds?"

The woman leaned over the counter. Her name tag said MADELINE MURPHY. "Pornography." She whispered the word, separating the syllables.

Agnes shook her head, hoping her expression mirrored Madeline's disgusted one. "Is Mr. Pasquali in?"

"He won't do a thing about it."

"I'll talk to him."

She paused at the computers, adjusted her belt, and hummed into the ear of one of the users. He was no one to be downwind from. A glance at the antics on the monitor screen made her want to call a cop.

The man turned, looking sheepish. Then he noticed the uniform and slid off the stool. "It's all yours."

"Get rid of the garbage."

He hit a key, and the screen went blank. The other scholars now noticed what was going on. Her uniform had the same effect on them.

"Which of you drives a 1999 Ford?"

They were almost flattered to be thought affluent enough to own an automobile, but one by one they drifted away, like the accusers of the woman taken in adultery. Agnes was born again and knew the wrath that was to come.

"They'll be back," Madeline said desolately.

"So where's Pasquali's office?"

The one with MR. FREDERICK PASQUALI on the door, as it happened. Agnes knocked, turned the knob, and walked in.

He was seated at his desk but turned toward his computer. He might have been one of the derelicts outside, except that on the screen was the Web site of the library. Finally he turned. At the sight of her, he started to rise, then remained seated. "What do you want, Officer?"

"We had a complaint."

"Oh my God. Look, Officer, there is nothing I can do about those damned computers. Ask anyone. It's a free country, damn it."

"I also wanted to thank you for the 911 call reporting the body of Ned Bunting in the river."

The statement might have flustered him. He might have got angry. He might have denied it. He did none of these things. He just stared. "How did you know?"

"Cell calls are recorded."

He thought about it, then nodded. "I suppose they are."

"You want to tell me about it?"

It was clear he didn't, but what could he do? He was silent for a time, preparing what he had to say. "It's a delicate matter, Officer. Do you know what that area is called?"

"Lovers' lane. An odd description of a parking area."

"I was with someone. We got out and took a walk, down to the river. That's when we saw the body. So I called 911."

"And got out of there?"

"Look, I did what any citizen should do. What more could I have done?"

"You thought he was dead?"

"He was dead."

"How could you tell?"

"It was obvious."

"You thought he had drowned?"

"I thought he was dead. I called 911."

"We figure the body was already dead when it was transported there, then dragged through the underbrush and thrown into the river."

Pasquali opened his hands. "How could I know that?"

"Who were you with?"

"I don't think you have a right to know that."

"It would have been hard for one person to carry a man that big, or drag him, even, to the river."

Pasquali leapt to his feet. "Now wait a minute."

"You're right. You should have a lawyer." She unhooked her phone and called Cy Horvath. "I've got him, Cy. What next? Okay, I'll wait right here." She hung up and looked around the office. "Nice place. You're going to miss it. What are those?" In the corner was a pile of folded plastic sheets.

"They wrapped the paintings we have here."

Now he got on the phone. "Gloria, Fred. Who was that lawyer you were telling me about? The one with the tweed hat. Get hold of him and tell him to come to my office immediately."

"Have him meet us downtown," Agnes advised. "Where is your car parked?"

"Don't you have one?"

"Oh, we'll be impounding yours. Who's Gloria?"

He became a Trappist; his lips were sealed. The little round bald spot on the crown of his head contributed to the impression. He had done all the talking he intended to do.

The first thing that had impressed Cy Horvath about Agnes was the fact that she drove Peanuts Pianone crazy. The second thing was that, although she had been hired in a gesture of affirmative action, she turned out to be a natural cop. When she phoned from Pasquali's office, he was waiting for the call. He might have told her to bring the librarian in, but it seemed wiser to go to the scene.

The first surprise when he entered the library was seeing at the checkout counter the woman who had accused Gregory Barrett of misconduct as a priest years ago. He showed her his identification and considered verifying who she was but decided he had better back up Agnes. "Mr. Pasquali's office," he said.

"The officer is in there with him."

"I know. Show me where it is."

And leave her post? Why not? As they passed the bank of computers, the woman said, "She cleared them all out of here."

"Ah."

The woman shook her head. "Day after day, they come in and spend hours looking at pornographic sites."

Then he remembered the complaints that came weekly, doubtless from this woman.

"Why should a library provide free Internet access?" Cy asked.

"Exactly!"

She moved on, and Cy followed her to Pasquali's door. "Thank you." He waited for her to leave, which she did with some reluctance. Then Cy opened the door and went in.

A mute head librarian sat at his desk, hands to his cheeks, eyes closed. Agnes was standing at ease near the door. She turned to Cy.

"He is the man who made the 911 call."

"Good work, Lamb."

He touched her arm and went to the desk. "I'm Lieutenant Horvath."

"I will say nothing until my lawyer is with me."

"Except that you will say nothing until your lawyer is with you? All right. I think we had better have our conversation downtown. Let's go."

"Is this an arrest?" Pasquali's eyes widened. "Are you putting me under arrest? What is the charge?"

"Why don't we wait until your lawyer joins you downtown?"

"I can refuse to go."

"Of course you can. Then we will arrest you."

"My God."

He rose as if his legs were unequal to the task. "I do this under protest."

Agnes opened the door, and Cy led Pasquali back to the main desk. Madeline Murphy looked at the procession of three with wonderment. Pasquali stopped at the desk but failed to find words to express his situation.

Agnes said, "Mr. Pasquali is coming downtown to help us with an investigation."

With that slim protection of his dignity, Pasquali walked at Cy's side to the front door.

"Who's your lawyer, Mr. Pasquali?"

"A man named Tuttle."

"Are you serious?"

"What's wrong?"

"Not a thing." If Cy had been a smiling man, he would have smiled. He wondered what expression Agnes wore. He turned to look. All her teeth were on display and her eyes sparkled. Tuttle!

Downtown, before Tuttle arrived, Cy had Agnes go over what they knew. Pasquali need say nothing, Cy told him. So Agnes presented her case.

Pasquali had made the 911 call from lovers' lane on the opposite side of the Fox River. He admitted it. This put him in a privileged position to help them find out what had happened to Ned Bunting. The body had been found in the river, but the man had died of a broken neck. That suggested he had been killed somewhere else and transported to the site. The suggestion was reinforced by the discovery of a large sheet of plastic that had been thrown into the weeds below the parking area. Tests were being made on it now. Of course, Mr. Pasquali's car would be examined—

It was then that Tuttle arrived, bustling, tweed hat on the back of his head, suit jacket open, expansive belly on display. He went immediately to Pasquali and laid a hand on his shoulder. "I want to be alone with my client."

"Of course. Agnes, take Mr. Pasquali and his lawyer to one of the visiting rooms upstairs."

"In the jail?" Tuttle cried. "Have you put this man under arrest?"

"Not yet."

Tuttle looked as if he would like to perform for his client, but even more he wanted to learn from Pasquali what was going on. He took his client away with Agnes as escort.

Cy went in to tell Phil Keegan what was happening. "You think he did it?"

"I don't think, I'm a cop."

"A librarian?"

"He's head of the branch that has been complaining about bums looking at pornography on their computers all day."

Phil shook his head. "I put it to Jacuzzi. He tells me there isn't anything that can be done about it."

"Funny thing, Phil. Madeline Murphy, the woman who accused Gregory Barrett, is a librarian there. She probably thinks we've taken Pasquali in for corrupting derelicts."

Agnes looked in. "I put them in a visiting room upstairs. I'm going back to the library, all right? I want to talk with the woman at the desk."

"Good idea." When she was gone, Cy said, "That is one good cop."

"Do we have any bad ones?"

As if in answer, Peanuts shuffled in. "Someone told me Tuttle was here."

"He's with a client."

"No kidding." Peanuts shuffled out. It would have been cruel to tell him what Agnes, his nemesis, had been up to while Peanuts was napping in the pressroom.

"By the way, Cy, Pippen left a message for you."

Phil found a note and handed it to Cy. It read like a telegram. "Tests are in. Positive."

On the day they discovered the body, after Fred had made the 911 call, he and Gloria had driven away, not speaking until they were a mile from the parking area. Gloria's horror had diminished enough for her to wonder what the appropriate reaction to this dreadful event should be. For several days, she had been enjoying the sensation of being fought over by two men.

Ned, after being laid out by Fred, had gone off to nurse his injured pride, but that night he had called. "I want to talk with you."

"We're talking." Gloria got comfortable, preparing to enjoy this.

Ned's voice trembled with anger. "Who was that bastard who attacked me?"

"A friend of mine. I think you attacked him first, Ned. He was only defending himself."

"I'm coming over."

"There's no point in that, Ned. Maddie and I are going out to dinner."

"I'll come along. I want to talk to her, too."

Having a witness to Ned's jealousy appealed. "Maybe I should call Fred and ask him along."

"He's the man who attacked me in front of your house, isn't he?"

Gloria still could not believe what she had seen Fred do.

"How in the world did you do to him what you did?" she had asked him.

"It's a simple maneuver. I have a black belt, you know," Pasquali replied.

"How would I know that?"

"Now you do. He hasn't bothered you since, has he?"

"Not since you've been so attentive."

He put out his hand and she took it.

She had also told Maddie about the way Fred had handled Ned Bunting when he threatened him in front of her house.

"Mr. Pasquali?"

"It was over before it began. He took Ned's hand and suddenly, whoops, Ned was flat on his back on the lawn."

"I would never have believed it," Madeline said.

Since he had insisted, Gloria had told Ned where she and Maddie were dining, the Great Wall. The helpings there were enormous. Whenever she ate there, Gloria brought two-thirds of what she had ordered home in Styrofoam containers, enough for several solitary meals.

They were already in their booth when Ned arrived, weaving among the tables like a man with a mission. He slid into the booth beside Madeline.

"We've already ordered, Ned." He seemed to have to remind himself he was in a restaurant. Maddie was studying him for signs of injury. "Gloria tells me you've met my boss."

"Have I?"

"Mr. Pasquali."

"The black belt," Gloria added.

"I have a good mind to bring charges against him, for assault."

"No one would blame you."

"You're my witness."

"Oh, I couldn't do that to Fred."

"Damn Fred!"

The waitress came, and he ordered shrimp fried rice. They would all drink hot tea.

The interruption enabled Ned to change the subject. He hunched toward Maddie. "Do you still have cold feet?"

Gloria laughed. "I had no idea you two knew one another so well."

Ned growled. To Maddie, he said, "I have drafted the story about Barrett."

"I don't want any more publicity."

Ned threw himself back. He glared at Maddie, and then his manner softened. "Things have gone too far. It's no longer yours to decide. And it's no longer your word against his. Tests can be made that will show that he is the father of your child."

"But what if he isn't?"

"Why would you say that?"

"Because he isn't."

"But . . ." Ned leaned forward, then sat back. "Tuttle found the records. It's a public matter."

"All those records prove is that he was of help to me in a very difficult period. You're the one who assumed it had another meaning."

"I assumed! You're the one that told the chancery office Barrett had abused you. Why would you do that if it hadn't happened?"

Madeline looked at Gloria. "We thought I had suppressed the memory."

Ned turned to Gloria. "She's as much as saying that you put the idea into her head."

"It sounds like you're the one putting ideas in people's heads."

Still, Gloria sympathized with Ned. After all, she was the one who had told him about Maddie, arranged for them to meet, and encouraged him to write about it. Then she remembered.

"That book you gave me? By Harry Austin? Tell him, Maddie."

"Harry Austin is a very prolific writer of trivial fiction, which is enormously popular."

"And you're not Harry Austin," Gloria said. "The library copies have the dust jackets, and his picture is on them."

"It was just a joke."

"That you're a writer?"

That was the unkindest cut of all. He slid out of the booth, rose to his full height, and looked down at Gloria as he had looked at her from the center aisle of St. Bavo's when she was seated in a pew—but the luster he'd had was dimmed.

"You, too, Gloria?"

And he left. Their orders came, and Gloria told the waitress to put Ned's in a Styrofoam box. With what she would take home of her own order, she would eat Chinese for a week.

Now, with Ned permanently out of the picture, she needed to talk to Fred. It had been a full day since they had agreed not to see one another for a time. When he didn't answer the phone in his office, she dialed again and asked for Maddie.

"Gloria, they just arrested Pasquali. The police marched him out the door."

Gloria listened patiently while Maddie developed her theory: Her complaints about the library computers were finally getting some results. Gloria thought otherwise. Ned must have brought charges against Fred, and they were being acted on posthumously. How weird.

Then that night on the news, she heard that Frederick Pasquali, head librarian of the Benjamin Harrison branch of the Fox River library, was taken in for questioning in the murder of Ned Bunting, a local writer.

8

When he was alone with Pasquali and had him seated at a table, Tuttle took off his hat, sat across from him, then put his hat on again. "Give me a dollar."

"What?"

"As a retainer. Then you're officially my client."

Pasquali got out his wallet and threw a dollar bill on the table.

Tuttle scooped it up and transferred it to his hat with a practiced gesture. "Who recommended me?"

"Gloria Daley mentioned your name. It just popped into my head when the police were grilling me."

"A fine woman. Now tell me what this is all about."

Tuttle was used to representing clients whose guilt was certain, but in the case of Pasquali he had assumed he had a respectable citizen requiring his services. Head librarian of the Benjamin Harrison branch. How much more respectable than that could you get? He began taking notes as Pasquali spoke, but had him start over because his ballpoint pen seemed to be writing in invisible ink. He shook it, made a few squiggles, and got it flowing.

The first item was that Fred Pasquali had made the 911 call reporting the body of Ned Bunting in the river.

"That's no crime."

"Crime! It was the act of a dutiful citizen."

Tuttle liked that. "So you found the body."

"Yes. I got out and walked down by the river and there it was."

"You called and left the area."

"Is that a crime?"

"Not that I know of. You were alone?"

"No, I was with someone."

"Who?"

"I'd rather not say."

Tuttle wiggled his nose and tapped it with his ballpoint. "That parking area is called lovers' lane."

"I know that."

"And you were with someone."

"It was in the middle of the afternoon."

"Time?"

"Three, a little after."

Tuttle made a note of it. "And this other person knows you made the call to 911?"

"Of course."

"Better tell me his name."

"*His* name! It was a woman."

"Gloria Daley?"

Pasquali lurched at the sound of the name. Tuttle felt that he had just pulled a Perry Mason. His elation was brief. He knew what Hamilton Burger would now spring on the jury. Tuttle had heard of Pasquali's laying out of Ned Bunting. Gloria had not been shy about telling the story of the two men vying for her affections.

"Jujitsu?" Tuttle had asked her, amused by the scene she described.

"I don't know what it's called, but you know what a big man Ned is. He made a threatening move and Fred just took his hand, flipped him, and laid him on the lawn."

Fred Pasquali could not keep secret that it was Gloria Daley he had been with and that he had been seen decking his rival with a deft and practiced movement of the martial arts. Things were looking bad for Pasquali—and good for Tuttle. A client in this kind of doodoo would run up quite a bill before he was tried and convicted and sent off to Joliet.

"How did you know it was Gloria?"

Tuttle tapped his head with the ballpoint. He was beginning to look tattooed. "When we go back to Horvath, let me do the talking. Is there anything else I should know?"

"Like what?"

"Did you kill Ned Bunting?"

"I never killed anyone in my life!"

"You did rough him up, though, didn't you?"

Pasquali's expression made it clear that he realized it was Gloria who had told the story. He waved his hand. "That doesn't matter. Gloria was with me Wednesday afternoon. She knows what happened, or didn't happen, then."

"She'll make a good witness," Tuttle said ambiguously.

When they went at it in Cy Horvath's office, it became clear that the police knew what Pasquali had done to Ned Bunting in front of Gloria Daley's house. Agnes Lamb had called it in from the Benjamin Harrison branch, where she had heard it from Maddie.

Then the plastic sheet was brought in. It seemed similar to those Agnes had seen at the library, those Gloria had wrapped her paintings in when she brought them for hanging. The plastic threatened to play a similar role here. A search warrant had been obtained and a police tow truck had been sent to bring in Pasquali's automobile. Tuttle attempted to smile away the damning items that had been mentioned.

"We have a witness, Horvath."

"His companion in lovers' lane?"

Pasquali began to say something, but Tuttle shut him off. "Her name is Gloria Daley. I suggest you talk with her and then let my client go."

Instead Cy had a discussion with the prosecutor, Jacuzzi. It was a slack period, and the prosecutor loved to be in court. Besides that, he thought they had sufficient reason for an arraignment.

"Aren't you going to talk to Gloria Daley first?" Tuttle asked.

"We already have."

Pasquali groaned.

So they went before a magistrate—Benny Jackson, deaf as a post—who officially decided to hold Frederick Pasquali under suspicion of having brought about the death of Ned Bunting.

"Will you set bail, Your Honor?"

"For a man accused of homicide?"

"He's not going anywhere. He wants to defend his good name. Mr. Pasquali is a librarian."

"He sounds like some sort of gymnast to me."

Still, bail was set, and Tuttle ushered his client out to his car. "Where do you want to go?"

"I'd like to just disappear."

"That would be expensive."

Pasquali asked Tuttle to drive him to the library, but on the way he changed his mind. "I'd better go home."

"Good idea."

"Wait, I have a better idea. Take me to Gloria."

For Phil Keegan, caught up now in the Ned Bunting murder, the results of the tests run on the materials that had been turned over to Dr. Pippen did not loom as large as they might have, but for Father Dowling this was extraordinary news indeed, and he arranged a meeting with Amos Cadbury to discuss the matter. Amos was as struck by the importance of those results as Father Dowling had been.

"You mean the results establish that the son of Madeline Murphy is also Gregory Barrett's son?"

"So I'm told."

"Does Barrett know?"

"I asked him to meet us here."

Amos winced. "I don't relish the prospect of telling him this."

"But how could it come as a surprise to him?"

Amos thought about that, then nodded slowly. "I see what you mean."

It was this that had assailed Roger Dowling ever since hearing from Phil Keegan that the DNA tests established a positive relationship between Gregory Barrett and Marvin Murphy. It was agreed that such testing put the question beyond doubt. Roger himself had made that point to Gregory Barrett, and now he found himself recalling that occasion, seeking in it any hint that Gregory had seen the testing as the definitive solution to the difficulty he had been put in by Madeline Murphy's accusations. He could recall no suggestion in Barrett's reaction that he feared such a test. Nor, for that matter, had he shown relief at the prospect of being vindicated by it. Had he known what the results would be? What would he say when confronted by them?

Gregory Barrett had arrived at Amos's office and been ushered in. There was anything but apprehension in his manner. "Have you heard?" he asked cheerfully.

Amos looked at Father Dowling. "Heard?"

"The woman has retracted her charges." He smiled. "God is good. Roger, I want you to say a Mass of thanksgiving for me. I won't pretend that this hasn't been one of the greatest trials of my life."

"Retracted the charges!" Amos was not given to outbursts, but his was an angry voice. In the light of the results of those tests, Roger could understand the patrician lawyer's reaction to Barrett's insouciance.

"I knew that my profession of innocence did not persuade you," Barrett said almost sadly to Cadbury. "I suppose I don't really blame you. It is the nature of such charges, particularly in the present atmosphere—"

Roger Dowling interrupted him. "Gregory, DNA tests have been run. The results show that you are the boy's father."

"That's impossible." He did not even raise his voice. He listened to Roger's account of what he had heard from Phil Keegan, shaking his head. "But where would they have gotten the materials to run such a test? They never asked me for anything. I'm afraid they've been duped."

Whatever reaction Roger Dowling had expected, it had not been this.

"Well?" Barrett asked. Now he was angry.

"Amos," Roger said, "may I use your phone?"

Within five minutes, he had arranged for Cy Horvath and Dr. Pippen to come to Amos Cadbury's office. As the three men waited, the atmosphere in Amos's office was tense. No one broke the silence but Gregory Barrett, once, when he said, "Do you believe this, Roger?"

"Greg, I am only reporting what I was told. When Lieutenant Horvath and Dr. Pippen arrive, you will confront the sources of that information."

The situation of Amos's office made the wait as short as possible—barely fifteen minutes, but it was an extremely long and trying quarter of an hour. The three men rose when Amos's secretary announced Dr. Pippen and Cy Horvath. The assistant coroner gave her hand to Amos, saying how delighted she was to meet him at last.

On any other occasion, Amos might have basked in her graciousness. "You have been asked here for a very particular reason, my dear. You know Father Dowling, I believe. This gentleman is Gregory Barrett. He has been under accusation—"

She nodded. "I know." Her eyes skimmed over Gregory and rested on Father Dowling.

"You know everyone, Lieutenant."

"Yes."

"Gregory Barrett has just learned of the results of the DNA

tests that were run. I wonder if you would describe them for us."

"Oh, I sent the materials out to a lab," Dr. Pippen said. Her head moved gracefully as she spoke, and her ponytail responded.

"What materials?" Barrett demanded.

"They were brought to me by Tuttle," Cy said.

"Tuttle! Good Lord. And where, pray, did he get them?"

"He said from your son, Thomas."

Barrett had spoken like one outraged, but at Cy's answer he lifted from his chair. "And you believed him?"

Suddenly it was Cy Horvath who was in the dock. His expression had remained unchanged since he came into Amos's office, and it did not alter under Barrett's questioning, but it was clear to Roger that Cy was thinking.

"Yes," he said at last. "I believed him. I turned the materials over to Dr. Pippen—"

"But this is preposterous. Why in the name of heaven would my son . . ." He turned to Roger. "Whatever this man Tuttle gave to Lieutenant Horvath, whatever Dr. Pippen sent out for testing, is what must be questioned here."

"You're right," Cy said.

"Of course I'm right. Has this story been made known publicly?"

"Only those of us in this room know the results," Cy assured him.

At the close of the meeting, Gregory Barrett had gained the respect of anyone who hitherto might have doubted him. Roger was particularly relieved—and could sense the discomfiture of Cy Horvath. The idea of simply accepting those materials on Tuttle's say-so was indeed preposterous to anyone who knew

Tuttle. Amos was clearly swayed when he found that Tuttle was at the bottom of this.

"That man . . ." he began, but did not go on.

Cy was eager to get onto the matter, but before he went, Barrett demanded, unnecessarily, that these alleged tests must be kept completely confidential. Cy accepted the criticism stoically. Before leaving, Dr. Pippen again took Amos's hand. He was now in a better mood to clasp it in both of his and thank her for coming on what must seem a fool's errand.

"Tuttle." The dean of the Fox River bar sighed, and shook his head.

Tuttle was not in the courthouse; he was not at the Great Wall; Peanuts was enjoying solitude and slumber in the pressroom. There was only one place left: Tuttle's office.

"I'll come with you," Agnes said.

"No. This is my goof, and I will correct it."

"If it's a goof."

Cy turned to her. "You think the son could have pulled some kind of trick?"

"I don't know him. He had to have something from the other kid, Marvin Murphy. How did he get it?"

"It was a toothbrush."

"Why don't I see what I can find out about that?"

Cy turned the car over to Agnes, since Tuttle's office was close enough to walk to. Besides, he needed to blow off steam. For a moment, Agnes had seemed to come up with a way out of this: Barrett's son plays a trick. Neither he nor Agnes knew the Barrett boy, but Cy knew Tuttle. Right now, he felt like taking the brim of that tweed hat and pulling it down to Tuttle's knees.

"Lieutenant Horvath!" Hazel cried when he arrived at her office. She also punched her phone, thus giving Tuttle two warnings.

Cy turned the knob of Tuttle's office and pushed. Nothing. "Unlock the door, Tuttle."

Half a minute later, the door opened. Tuttle was studying its hinges when Cy went in. "Must have stuck. Probably never been oiled."

Cy looked around the office. It looked like a rat's nest. There were a couple of bookshelves, but all the books were tipped at an angle or lay flat, some still open. Atop them was a replica of the Statue of Liberty, Styrofoam boxes from the Great Wall, a diploma attesting to Isaac Tuttle's graduation from law school, and a series of framed photographs, mostly of a man who bore a resemblance to Tuttle.

"The paternal parent," Tuttle said over Cy's shoulder.

"I thought it was your father." Cy removed newspapers and other debris from a chair and sat. "We got a positive result from the DNA test."

"That ought to change her mind."

"You don't seem surprised."

"Man that is born of woman . . ." Tuttle began, but let it go. He didn't know the ending anyway.

"You think Madeline Murphy will change her mind and accuse him again?"

"If she takes a good lawyer's advice."

"How many sides of the street are you working, Tuttle? Tell me about the envelopes you dumped on my desk."

Tuttle was in his chair now, one arm of which looked broken. He jiggled with it as he sat. "They were dumped on this very desk, Horvath. By young Barrett."

"He just dropped by and handed them over to you."

"His father had been here before him, you know. Several weeks ago. I suppose he heard me discussed at home."

"And he still came?"

"Ho ho."

"Gregory Barrett questions the whole thing. We had a session at Amos Cadbury's office. I was in the embarrassing position of having to admit that I had been trusting you in the matter. Why would his son bring you materials that turn out to incriminate his father?"

"Because he thought they would have the opposite effect. He is a splendid young man, Cy. Devoted to his father." Tuttle's eye traveled to the photographs on the wall. "I understand he will be going to Notre Dame in the fall."

"Didn't they used to have a football team?"

"They'll be back. They'll be back."

"How did this splendid young man explain how he had got hold of those materials?"

"What's the problem? The house would be full of things he might have chosen."

"His father's things?"

"Yes. There was a Band-Aid, for example, rescued from a wastebasket in his parents' bathroom. Gregory Barrett had cut his finger."

"And what did he have from Madeline's son, Marvin?"

"Just a toothbrush."

"Did he say how he got it?"

Tuttle thought about it. He was beginning to see the problem. "No."

"What do you suppose he would have said if you asked him where he got it?"

"Good question."

"I should have asked it before."

"As should I, Cy. Do you think we've been had?"

"You know the kid, I don't."

Tuttle adjusted his tweed hat. "I will find out."

"Don't bother. Agnes Lamb is on it."

Tuttle left his hat at the angle it was. "Much better. How will this affect the case against my client, I wonder."

"Pasquali? You're the lawyer. It says so on that diploma."

"I'll get him off."

"Sure you will."

Hazel simpered at him when he emerged from the inner office. "Honestly, this place is getting as busy as Grand Central Station."

"I've never been there," Cy said, and kept on going.

He might have told Tuttle the results of the examination of Pasquali's car. The plastic sheet that had been found at the scene had definite signs of having held the body of Ned Bunting, but there was nothing in Pasquali's car to tie the plastic to it. His trunk was jammed full: golf clubs, two pairs of golf shoes, jogging shoes, and a very sweaty sweat suit. There wasn't room there for the plastic, let alone a body. Nor was there anything inside the car to indicate that Pasquali and his girlfriend had hauled the dead body of Ned Bunting to the river and dumped it in.

Agnes Lamb was in an unmarked car. After parking, she sat for a while looking at the house in which the woman who had caused such a stir lived with her son. She would be at the library, no doubt. During their conversation on the day Pasquali was taken in for questioning, Agnes had been told about the son, Marvin. He sounded like someone only a mother could love, a drone who lazed about the house all day. Well, let's find out.

She was in uniform, which maybe was a good thing. The combination of her race and the uniform and all the appurtenances of a guardian of the law gave an unmistakable advantage. She pressed the bell and then stood back from the door, the better to be visible from within. A minute went by, then two. She rang again. And again. Then she went around back, and there was Marvin sunning himself, with a beer within reach. Agnes got between him and the sun. His eyes opened, and then he tried to sit up, not so successfully.

"Marvin?"

"Who are you? What is this?" The uniform was having its effect.

"Just a few questions."

He was in a seated position now, his hands dangling between his knobby knees. He was in swimming trunks, and his upper body glistened with oil. He put a towel around his shoulders. "Questions about what?"

"I've already spoken with your mother."

He groaned and lifted his hands as if in prayer. "She said she was going to drop all that."

"Don't you want to know who your father was?"

"I know who he was. He was a sailor. I can show you pictures."

"Do you know Thomas Barrett?"

"Barrett. His name isn't Thomas."

"This is his son."

Marvin might have been saluting, the way he shaded his eyes. "I heard he has a son."

"At least one."

"Oh, come on. Not even my mother believes that story. She was talked into it by Mrs. Daley." He thought. "The Barrett kid did call me."

"Did you get together?"

"What for? It's all over."

"Have you ever heard of DNA tests?"

He shrugged.

"A DNA test has been run," she went on. "The results were positive. Do you know what that means?"

"Sure. Don't rely on tests. How could they run one, anyway? They'd have to have something from me."

"They did. A toothbrush."

He laughed. "How would anyone get hold of my toothbrush?"

"It's not missing?"

"No, it is not missing." He smiled. "I brushed my teeth an hour ago."

"Show me."

"Take a look."

"I don't mean your teeth. Show me your toothbrush."

"You're serious."

"I'm serious."

He got to his feet, not very agilely, and started for the house. She followed him inside. He seemed almost naked in the house. Apparently he felt the same way; the first thing he did when he went into the bathroom was put on a robe. Then he handed her a toothbrush.

"This is yours."

"Of course it's mine."

"You just have the one?"

"Why would I need more than one toothbrush?"

"You're not missing a toothbrush?"

Agnes felt that she had found what she had come for. If someone was playing a trick, it wasn't Marvin.

"Your mother said you're taking courses online."

"In computing science. If I didn't already know what they're teaching me, I couldn't take the course. Would you like a beer?"

"Sure, but I won't take one. I'm on duty."

"Tracking down toothbrushes?"

"Did you floss? There's a law, you know."

It took him a while to realize she was kidding. She thanked him and said her colleagues would want him to repeat what he had told her.

"It's important?"

"We think so."

In the car, she got hold of Cy and told him what she had learned.

"It looks like we've been had," he said.

"What next?"

"The Barrett boy. Thomas. We'll go together."

Perhaps because she had described it so vividly to several people, the image of Fred Pasquali taking Ned Bunting's hand, turning away, and then wheeling the tall man through the air and depositing him unceremoniously on her lawn was etched into Gloria Daley's memory. After the horror of the discovery of Ned's body in the shallow waters along the shore of the Fox River, her emotions had been in such a turmoil that she had scarcely time to realize that Ned Bunting, whose commanding presence in the center aisle of St. Bavo's had fascinated her, was no more. Dead. She shivered at the realization now.

On the way back to town, Fred had suggested that they must not see one another for a few days and should talk to no one, and she had agreed. In the time since, strange thoughts had occurred to her.

Why had he driven to the parking area known for years as

lovers' lane? It was only the third time that they had been alone together. She remembered looking up through the window in the roof of his car and seeing the weeping willows swaying. His arm had crept around her shoulders. Was it she who had suggested that they walk by the river? She had spent so much time going over Maddie's memories of long ago, helping her friend recall what she had driven from her mind, and now she found that her own short-term memory was unreliable. Then the dark thoughts came.

Fred had known that Ned Bunting's body was in the river. He had taken her there deliberately so that she could discover the corpse. She found herself imagining him dealing more decisively with Ned than he had in front of her house, killing him, and then taking the body to the river, perhaps only an hour or so before he had driven to the parking area with her. If something like that had happened, she was his alibi. Of course he had tried to keep her name out of the investigation—that would have been part of the plan—but he must have realized that eventually it would become known that she had been with him, and then her account would effectively exonerate him.

The trouble with such thoughts was that they were difficult to entertain when she and Fred were once more together. Fred was free on bail and had asked to be taken immediately to her. All her dark thoughts vanished when she opened the door to him. So short a time ago, she had had two competing admirers. Now she had only Fred. She opened her arms to him, and he trembled as she drew him close.

"I have never had such an experience in my life," he whispered.

"There, there."

She offered him coffee, but he wanted something more bracing. "It's early for grappa."

"Grappa is what I need."

So they sat on her couch, sipping the potent liquid, while he told her what he had been through downtown.

"Tuttle? Why did you call him?"

"You had mentioned him. The name just occurred to me. How many lawyers do I know?"

"He hasn't much of a reputation."

"I can believe it."

"You can always change lawyers."

"Even Tuttle should be able to handle this. The charge is ridiculous."

"Of course it is."

"Have you any idea who could have done such a thing?"

"I?"

"You knew him. Who were his friends? Who were his enemies?"

There was no point in mentioning Monsignor Sledz of St. Bavo's. "He hated Quirk. He hated Gregory Barrett."

"But did they hate him?"

"I'm afraid that they thought him a figure of fun."

"Oh, let the police figure out who did it."

He had finished his grappa and wanted more. It was now twilight, and she was not sure she wanted a drunk Fred Pasquali in her living room. It seemed important to change the subject, so she told him about the odd conjunction of events: Maddie had decided not to pursue her accusations; she had forbidden Ned Bunting to write about her.

"How did he react to that?" Fred asked.

"He didn't think it much mattered anymore what she wanted or didn't want. Now, Tuttle tells me that DNA tests have actually been run."

"That should settle it."

"But how?"

"Either way, the police should arrest him."

"Gregory Barrett?"

"Who had better motive?"

Gloria would have preferred a vengeful lover rather than the object of Maddie's accusations. Fred's arm had crept around her shoulders. She was about to shrug it off when the promised consolations changed her mind. She turned to him, looking directly into his eyes, then lifted her face to his.

Tetzel of the *Tribune* spent much of his day in the courthouse, in the pressroom for the most part. Shreds and scraps of information came to him from the courts, from police headquarters, and in the obiter dicta of politicians, grist enough for him to grind from his computer those authoritative pieces on the affairs of Fox River, Illinois, that had earned him the respect of a large number of readers, if not of his editors and fellow journalists. The latter, like the subjects of his world-weary and omniscient pieces, knew that what Tetzel wrote concerned an imaginary world, a world largely of his own creation. Fiction, of a sort. There were even those who knew of the efforts at a novel stored away on his hard disk, little bursts that never exceeded a thousand words. Real fiction had proved more demanding than journalism.

Of course, having retained a modicum of self-knowledge, he was his own severest critic; no need to feed the jealousy and envy of his fellows in the craft. He himself knew how flimsy was the basis of his reputation. There were even days when he resolved to engage in the kind of serious reporting he had dreamt of doing in his youth. Such a desire arose with new strength as he picked up bits and pieces of the local version of the clerical scandals that were, in the tired phrase, rocking the bark of Peter, or chipping the rock of Peter, or . . . It was when he was eavesdropping on the ineffable Tuttle that he first heard of the DNA tests allegedly being run to settle the charge that had been brought against Gregory Barrett.

No need to say that the arrival of Barrett on the local scene, his much touted program on NPR, and the pieces he was occasionally prevailed upon to contribute to the *Tribune*'s Sunday book page filled Tetzel with mixed emotions. His own reputation had made him skeptical of the reputations of others. Feet of clay must inhabit the highly shined loafers that carried Barrett like a winged Mercury through the Chicago celebrity stratosphere.

The charges against him were rumors of an elusive kind, difficult to fashion into the sort of all-knowing report that was Tetzel's trademark. So he had bided his time. That Tuttle seemed to be privy to things hidden from him took the sheen from the rumors, and when the impossibly inept Ned Bunting had been admitted to the sacrosanct pages of the *Tribune* with a piece on Roger Dowling that would never have made it into the high school offerings that appeared once a week, Tetzel was dismayed. Quirk, of course, disclaimed all responsibility, but Bunting was said to be the confidant of the woman who had brought charges against Gregory Barrett—who, to Tetzel's surprise, turned out to be a laicized priest of the Chicago archdiocese and who, upon his defection, had descended into the lowlands of southern Illinois, where he had improbably attained the fame that had eventually brought him back to the area. As an instance of clerical scandal, this had the marks of the anomalous.

Barfield, the lawyer for the archdiocese in these matters, would tell Tetzel nothing that could provide a basis for even one of his imaginative pieces. The woman had allegedly refused compensation from the archdiocese, but this Barfield refused to confirm. If so, what was she up to? Enter the dreadful Ned Bunting. It began to look like something Tetzel would not go near with a twelve-foot pole. Still, he was child enough of his time to be stirred by the thought that an objective test, a scientific test, could decide the matter, and so he had gone to work.

The lovely Dr. Pippen in the coroner's office had proved susceptible to his flattery and curiosity. "Of course, it wasn't the sort of thing I myself could do," she had said.

"That difficult?"

"That different from what we do here."

"Ah." Tetzel did not want to think of the things done there in the morgue. How had such a dream of a woman gotten involved in so ghoulish an enterprise?

She was a medical doctor married to a medical doctor. "Obgyn," she explained.

He let it go. It was part of his professional manner never to reveal his ignorance. "So who ran the tests?"

A laboratory right here in Fox River, as it happened. Pippen added that she probably shouldn't be telling him all this. He assured her it was only deep background, and he left her with the name of Fenwick Labs. A sense of destiny came upon him when he remembered that Larson, a serious drinker and sometime companion in alcoholic revels, worked at Fenwick.

Tetzel found him bellied up to the bar of the Tempest and elbowed his way in beside him. "Let's sit in the corner so I can buy you a drink."

"I've got a drink."

"I meant the next one."

Like Pippen, Larson was a person of great professional propriety. Pippen had only the pardonable weakness of a woman, but Larson's Achilles' heel was a debility Tetzel shared. The juice of the grape—or more literally, single malt scotch—made Larson vulnerable to Tetzel's subtle inquisitiveness, but patience was the watchword. An hour and a half had passed before Tetzel asked, as if out of the blue, what Larson thought of DNA testing.

"Personally, it sounds to me on a par with consulting the entrails of birds," the reporter said.

"Not at all, my dear fellow. Not at all."

"But in these circus trials of recent years, so-called experts on the matter have disagreed profoundly."

"There is no possibility of disagreement if the test is done correctly."

"Have you yourself ever done such a test?"

"Strange that you should ask."

The test Larson described was without doubt the one that interested Tetzel: a Band-Aid on the one side, a toothbrush on the other. "More than sufficient."

"For what?"

"A match."

"Positive?"

"Beyond dispute."

"Do you have time for another?"

Does the bear sleep in the woods?

It was early in the morning when Tetzel sat down at his computer in the pressroom of the courthouse. At that hour, he had the place to himself. Was this how Woodward and Bernstein had felt when they recounted the confidences of Deep Throat? They were probably sober when they wrote—all kinds of types got into journalism nowadays—but Tetzel had been careful to nurse his drinks as he sat with Larson, keeping refills for the intrepid scientist coming. When he rose to go, Larson said he might have a nightcap. It was certain he had a snoot full. Tetzel, on the other hand, found his mind sharpened by the relatively small amount he had drunk. His fingers were a little rubbery on the keyboard, causing any number of mishits and typos, but with spell check he could clean them up in a trice. And so he began, conscious that what he was writing was many levels above his ordinary output.

He finished a draft of the story; he honed and refined it. He printed it out and with one eye closed read it critically. He sat back. Like God in Genesis, he saw that what he had made was good. He sent it as an e-mail attachment to Quirk and went home to a bed that had a tendency to spin. He had suggested a headline, always risky with Quirk: GREGORY BARRETT PROVED FATHER OF ACCUSER'S SON.

14

Gregory Barrett reread *Huckleberry Finn* at least once a year, and he was rereading it now. As the raft on which Huck and Jim were floating to freedom neared Cairo, Illinois, Barrett held the book open against his chest and found himself wishing that he had stayed in Cairo. His apparent good fortune in being invited to move to the Chicago area had been no more than apparent. His program was now heard from coast to coast on the publicly supported network, so the promise that had brought him back home had proved true, but his return now threatened to be his undoing.

A woman he could not remember accused him of sexual misbehavior while he was still a priest. The woman had heard him on the air and, she had told Barfield, the archdiocesan lawyer in these matters, suddenly drew forth from the darkness of memory horrible events she had suppressed. She had dismissed with disdain the suggestion that she receive compensation and let bygones be bygones. The accusation, never made quite public, ticked like a time bomb that must surely eventually explode. Nancy knew him better than any other human being, and he could see the effect the accusation had had on her. So he had gone to see his old classmate Roger Dowling.

What a basis for an otherwise pleasant reunion! He had always liked Roger, and liked him more when he saw how he had emerged from his own difficulties. St. Hilary's seemed to Barrett the kind of parish they had dreamed of having during their seminary years. Roger had been wonderfully reassuring. If only the matter could be kept on such a humane basis. But Barfield had insisted that he see Amos Cadbury, an unpleasant duty made more tolerable by Roger Dowling's involvement. Barrett could tell, though, that neither the venerable dean of the Fox River bar nor his canon-lawyer classmate could see any easy way out of the matter.

Then the charge, Barfield informed him, had been made more serious still: He was accused of fathering the woman's child. Whether wisely or not, Barrett had enlisted the support of the seedy Tuttle, in the shameful hope that he could find some compensating dirt about his accuser. What Tuttle had turned up was records that increased Barrett's difficulty. To his horror, he found that now he could remember the woman and those long-ago events. What he had done then had been the right thing to do, and it seemed Kafkaesque that his sympathetic pastoral help was now turned against him.

Roger Dowling had surprised him by suggesting that this was actually a turn for the better: A charge of parentage was one that could be put to the test. In the event, the test seemed unnecessary. The woman, surprisingly, withdrew her charge. Prayers were indeed sometimes answered. He could feel the relief in Nancy when he held her in his arms.

Thomas said, "They should make the tests anyway. She might change her mind again."

That was not something Barrett was inclined to insist on. The testing could remain a possibility that would protect him if indeed she did change her mind.

Tests had been made, though, and tests whose result claimed that he was indeed the father of that woman's son. When he had gone to Amos Cadbury's office, he had assumed that it would be a session where his liberation would be celebrated. He recalled the psalm, said so often in his clerical days, *Laqueus contritus est, et liberati sumus.* The trap has been sprung, and we are freed. Instead he had walked into the most incredible claim of all.

"But that's impossible."

He could see how his words affected Amos Cadbury. What had the man expected, a shamefaced admission that he had been lying all along, that of course he was the most loathsome of men, a priest who had traded on the trust and confidence of a confused young woman for his own selfish ends, got her with child, and arranged for the whole burden to be put upon her? Did anyone believe he was capable of such a thing, or at least had been? His angry reaction had turned the day, and it was the testing itself that came under scrutiny. When Horvath arrived, Barrett could almost sympathize with the spot the lieutenant was in, a spot just vacated by himself, but Tuttle! Everyone in the room immediately recognized that Tuttle's involvement with the so-called evidence tainted it—and then to say that he had received the stuff from Thomas!

He had not told Nancy of the meeting in Amos Cadbury's office. He wanted Thomas to have the same opportunity he had

had, to dismiss the claim out of hand. What would Thomas have had to do with Tuttle?

Thomas was at a reception given for prospective Notre Dame students at a suburban hotel. It was now nearly midnight. Nancy had gone to bed; Gregory sat up with *Huckleberry Finn*, awaiting the return of his son, not wanting to go to bed before he had given Thomas the opportunity to laugh away the charge that had been made against him.

Of course, the charge was impossible. He would not doubt his son as others had doubted him, as if even the most preposterous accusation should carry more weight than the absence of any basis for it.

The headlights from the car swept past the study windows when Thomas turned in the driveway. Greg resumed reading, listening to the garage door open and then close. It made an awful racket in the night. The kitchen light was switched on, the refrigerator opened, and in a minute Thomas appeared in the doorway of the study.

"Still up?" he asked his father.

"Did you have a good time?"

Thomas yawned. "Wonderful. They showed a film. *Rudy*."

"Sit down for a minute."

"That's about as long as I'll last."

"Okay. I'll just give you a quick version of a meeting I was called to today."

It was a quick version. He felt that he could reduce it to thirty words or less: charge of parentage now backed up by DNA testing. He had finished the short form and taken a deep breath, about to go on, when Thomas spoke.

"And someone wondered where the materials for such a test had been found?" He had sat in the desk chair and turned it toward his father.

"Yes."

"I gave them to Tuttle, Dad. I collected the stuff and took it to him. You said what Father Dowling's reaction was to her second accusation. Now it can be proved. Well, why wait—"

"Tom, those tests purport to show that I am the father of that woman's son."

"All they can show is that you're the father of your son. I gave them my toothbrush, along with a used Band-Aid you had thrown in your wastebasket, from that little cut you had."

"But why?"

"Dad, it was like a problem on the SATs. The point had been reached when all seemed lost. Scientific tests would establish the truth beyond all possible doubt. What to do? Undermine confidence in the tests. The way you described Tuttle, I was sure he would take the bait, but whether he could convince anyone—"

"You deliberately prompted those tests with materials that would guarantee a positive match."

"And then when all the whooping and hollering begins, I come forward and say, 'Hey, that was my toothbrush. You've just proved I'm my father's son.' Imagine the reaction. Who's going to suggest another test?"

Tom looked at him brightly, the beginning of a smile, waiting to be congratulated. After a moment, Gregory opened his arms, and his son gave him a big bear hug. Against his father's shoulder, he said, "I'm almost sorry now that it was all for nothing." Tom stood. "I thought I was being so shrewd."

"Oh, you were shrewd, all right. Go to bed."

Then he was alone. He had thought that the nadir had been reached several times before, but this was a subbasement indeed. He lit a cigarette and immediately put it out. He would quit smoking. Maybe he would go on bread and water. But he sat on, alone, pensive. The only thought he had was that his own son had assumed he was guilty as charged.

In the morning, it became clear that what Tom had done could not remain a semiprivate joke. The story was on the front page.

GREGORY BARRETT PROVED FATHER OF ACCUSER'S SON.

❧ Part Four ❧

There was unseemly celebration in the pressroom when Tetzel's scoop was revealed to have been based on a fraud. Quirk had listened patiently as Tetzel explained the investigative reporting that had gone into his piece, the careful checking.

"It is nothing but facts!" Tetzel insisted.

"You've been had, Tetzel." Then, in an uncharacteristic addendum, "We've been had."

Quirk offered him the opportunity to expose the phony test, but for a time Tetzel demurred. The thought of explaining in authoritative detail how he had been duped did not appeal. Still, better he do it than someone else. The piece he wrote was relegated to an inner page, in the manner of a minor correction of an earlier story. It carried no byline, and Tetzel did not complain. In the courthouse pressroom, it was assumed that Quirk had written the retraction.

"You should have come to me," Tuttle said to him, almost sorry for his old foe. "I feel half responsible."

"That is a new high for you."

"Now, now. What is the word? Magnanimity. You will find it discussed by Aristotle."

"How the hell would you know?"

Tuttle had seen it on the Web, but there seemed no need to tell Tetzel that he was not relying on primary sources.

The question was, what, if anything, should he, Tuttle, do about it? Tetzel had painted himself into a corner, but young Barrett had deliberately used Tuttle as an instrument of his deception. To say that the little lawyer was disillusioned did not approach the letdown he felt. The clear implication of what Thomas Barrett had done was to incriminate his father—and yet, apparently, he had admitted everything to his father. Gregory Barrett did not return Tuttle's calls. No matter. His hands were full with the unfortunate Pasquali. Gloria Daley was proving to be a slender reed on which to rest his defense.

"Of course, the body had already been put in the river when we went up to that parking area," she said.

"Lover's lane."

"I wish you wouldn't call it that."

"Everyone calls it that."

The conversation took place after the obsequies for Ned Bunting the day before, presided over by Monsignor Sledz. "Late?" Monsignor Sledz cried. "He was never late. Edward Bunting was the most punctual man in the world. A true son of the parish." He put back his head and looked at the ornate ceiling of his church, as if seeking inspiration. Tuttle tuned him out. He knew all about Sledz and Ned Bunting. The pastor had driven the man to St. Hilary's.

Tuttle expressed some surprise at the venue of the funeral to Gloria Daley. From behind a black veil, she sighed. "He insisted on it. Father Dowling, of course, did not contest his prior rights. I regard it as a belated apology to Ned."

The funeral cortege had wound its way to the cemetery, and Tuttle had caught up with Gloria as they all moved away from the grave, having each sprinkled a few drops of holy water on the casket that would be lowered into the ground after all had withdrawn.

"I don't see Madeline."

"She couldn't get away. The responsibility for the Benjamin Harrison branch has fallen entirely on her shoulders."

"Pasquali will be exonerated, I guarantee you."

She lifted her veil and looked at him. "You're sure he's innocent?"

"As a babe!" He peered at her. "Aren't you?"

"Let me tell you the awful thought that occurred to me."

Tuttle looked over both shoulders as he listened to her, not wanting anyone else to hear her fantastic story about Fred Pasquali killing Ned, taking the body to the river, and then driving to the very spot with Gloria.

"We had never gone there before," she said.

"I thought you and Ned were an item."

She smiled as if from some eminence. "How quaint a phrase that is. But be that as it may, Fred and I were close."

"You say he had never taken you to lovers' lane before?"

She looked at him sadly. "Have you ever been in love?"

"Tell me about it."

"Sometimes I think it is an indiscriminate feeling that can be directed almost at will at a variety of objects."

"Ned or Fred?"

"If you will." She looked speculatively at Tuttle.

"You and Maddie and those two could have made a foursome."

"That was my initial thought. Of course, Maddie saw all of Fred she wanted to see at work. She blamed him for the vagrants who commandeered those computers." She paused. "Surely there can't be such dreadful things available on the Internet."

Tuttle himself had taken a peek from time to time, and almost immediately cleared the screen—but once having activated such a site, he found that it returned unbidden at awkward moments. He had first learned this when Hazel let out a shriek. He ran into her office. She had pushed back from her computer, a hand over her mouth. With the other she pointed.

Tuttle rushed over and cleared the screen. "Not during working hours," he said.

"I was writing a letter. It just suddenly jumped up." Hazel would have sympathized with Madeline's reaction to the use to which the library computers were put by slack-jawed, unshaven men who reeked of body odor.

Her own had been comparable when Pasquali arrived at Tuttle's office to discuss strategy later that day. She nodded and looked at the client with a hangman's eyes, and Tuttle hurried Pasquali into his inner sanctum.

"But I have an alibi, Tuttle. I've been thinking." Tuttle sat forward. "Gloria. We were together."

Tuttle sat back, taking the precaution of gripping his desk first so that his chair would not get out of control and head for the wall behind him. "Yes, yes. We already know that."

"We were there together. She was the one who saw the body first."

"But the body was already in the water."

"Of course it was in the water. How else could we have found it there?"

"How long had you been with her?"

"I picked her up and we went for a drive."

"Not too long before the discovery?"

Pasquali made an impatient noise. "What difference does that make?"

"Where were you before you picked Gloria up?"

Pasquali saw the point of the question and sat back, staring at Tuttle. *Et tu,* Tuttle? "Do you think I killed that man?"

"In court, they will tell you to answer the question."

"I was in church."

"Church!"

"I was saying a novena, praying that everything would go right with Gloria and me."

"What church?"

"St. Hilary's. She had been going there, and I thought the novena would be more effective there." Pasquali looked over Tuttle's head as he spoke. "I don't have to say this, do I?"

"It would help if someone saw you in church."

Pasquali thought. "There was some woman there all the time I was, a real busybody. She prowled along the side aisle as if she thought I was going to raid the poor box."

"Marie Murkin!" Tuttle cried.

"I don't know her name."

Tuttle was scribbling on a piece of paper. The body had been found at maybe three in the afternoon on Wednesday. If Pasquali was telling the truth, he would have been on his knees in St. Hilary's at, say, two o'clock. Maybe earlier. How long did a novena take?

"Nine days," Pasquali answered.

"I mean each time."

"Do you know who that woman was?"

"I'll look into it." He corrected himself. "We'll look into it."

When they left Tuttle's office, Hazel moved the stand on which her computer stood, getting it between herself and the door of the inner office. Her eyes narrowed as she looked at Pasquali. Tuttle wouldn't have wanted her on the jury.

Tuttle drove them to St. Hilary's, where he directed his car onto the onetime playground behind the school. Old men and women were wandering about over the tarmac surface. Because the number of children in the parish had dropped, the school had been turned into a gathering place for the elderly of the parish. They got out of the car, and at the sound of the doors closing, old people whose hearing was not impaired turned to stare at them. Tuttle doffed his tweed hat, took Pasquali's arm, and led him along the walk to the rectory. He went up the stairs to the kitchen door, Pasquali at his side, and knocked. He was about to knock again when the door opened.

"That's her!" Pasquali cried.

Mrs. Murkin looked at Pasquali and then at Tuttle. "What is this?"

"Do you recognize this man?"

"What has he done?"

"He's been praying a novena in the church here."

Marie Murkin had come out on the porch and was circling Pasquali. It was obvious to Tuttle that she remembered him. Marie nodded. "Yes, I've seen him in church."

Pasquali grabbed her hands and began kissing them. Marie danced away, flustered, but not really minding it. Tuttle had half a mind to kiss her himself.

Father Dowling heard the commotion on the back porch and put down the *Purgatorio*. At this hour of the day, when he wasn't reading Dante, he was reading Thomas Aquinas. The back door opened, there were voices in the hallway, and then Marie ushered in Tuttle and a man Father Dowling recognized from the photo that had run in the *Tribune*.

"Mrs. Murkin is Mr. Pasquali's alibi," Tuttle said triumphantly.

Father Dowling listened to Tuttle's account of the matter, with Pasquali nodding vigorously through the narrative. "The power of prayer," the priest murmured with a smile.

"He was praying that Gloria Daley would love him," Tuttle explained.

Marie lifted her shoulders, made a sound, and was about to leave.

"Is all this true, Marie?" Roger Dowling asked.

"Of course it's true."

"Then you are indeed Mr. Pasquali's alibi."

Half an hour later, when Tuttle and his client had left, Marie came in to him. "He kissed my hands when I recognized him."

"Regular confessions are on Saturday afternoon."

"He'll be lucky if his prayers aren't answered. Gloria Daley is the woman Ned Bunting was coming here to Mass with. I know all about her from Barbara Blaisdel at St. Bavo's."

"Don't be a sore loser, Marie."

When Phil Keegan came over that evening, Father Dowling told him what had happened.

"Oh, I heard. Tuttle has been spreading it all around the courthouse. Jacuzzi is blaming our investigation for not turning this up."

"Will charges be dropped?"

"If Tuttle stops crowing. Jacuzzi thought we had Pasquali nailed."

"So who killed Ned Bunting?"

Phil puffed on his cigar. Then, studying the books at his side, he said, "Agnes Lamb has a theory."

"What is it?"

"I hate theories. With Pasquali, it wasn't just a theory. The guy had fought with Bunting. They were apparently interested in the same woman."

"Gloria Daley."

"A real yo-yo."

"Meaning?"

"She's well into her fifties, maybe more, and she acts like a teenager. She paints."

"Her face?"

"Pictures. Watercolors. Oils. She's a factory. Apparently she has a house full of them. Pasquali has some of them hung in his branch library. That was the connection with Bunting, art."

"Ah."

"According to Cy, she giggles when she talks about Pasquali and Bunting. Like a girl. She's got the attention span of a fruit fly. She's the one who convinced Madeline Murphy that Gregory Barrett had taken advantage of her and was the father of her child."

"Which she no longer says."

"Now she's mad at the Daley woman for getting her into such a mess."

One of the effects of Tetzel's big story and its sheepish retraction was to make all accusations against priests seem manufactured. Barfield had been interviewed on television and came close to saying this, with the result that the archdiocesan settlement with a group of victims was suddenly in trouble. At least for Gregory Barrett, the results seemed just. His reaction in Amos Cadbury's office when he was told of the test poor Tetzel had broadcast to the world had convinced Roger Dowling that his old classmate was indeed a victim.

Amos Cadbury had come to dinner at the rectory the night before and had praised Marie's cooking to the skies. Marie wasn't above a little giggling herself. It was only later, in the study, that they had reviewed recent events.

Amos, like Father Dowling, was unhappy with the consequences of the ruse young Thomas Barrett had wrought. "I don't like being the Grand Inquisitor, Father, but there are some deeds that cry out to heaven for punishment. The way in which wayward priests were treated simply defies understanding. Complaints were brought, and a man was transferred to another parish, where he repeated his offense. And this went on and on, until it was decided to send him off for psychological counseling. Psychological counseling! As if something other than a grievous sin had been committed. Such men should have been dismissed from the priesthood!"

"You're preaching to the choir, Amos."

"It has been one of the heaviest professional crosses I have had to bear to see the way in which alleged psychological experts make mincemeat out of the notion that we are responsible for our deeds. But for the Church to treat bad priests as if they simply need some sort of mental tinkering and then all would be well! Sometimes I think I have lived too long."

"And now we hear of zero tolerance by bishops. As if they haven't been a large part of the problem."

"Cardinal Law."

"Yes. Bishops inherited problems when they took over a diocese and then fell into the same dodging practice."

"One would expect the churches to empty."

"Would one?"

Amos's cigar was eight inches long and had acquired an ash of almost an inch. He flicked it into the ashtray. "No, of course not."

"Religion is for sinners, after all."

"How could a man go on functioning as a priest when all the time . . ."

Father Dowling nodded. It was the most horrifying aspect of this scandal. A man who was engaged in the most reprehensible practices went on saying Mass, preaching, hearing confessions. The horror was not diminished by realizing how small the number of such priests was compared to the priesthood as a whole. They had brought down opprobrium on their innocent brothers. Who could blame the media for salivating at such evidence of duplicity?

"Can you imagine the conversation Gregory Barrett had with his son?" Amos asked.

"I'll be seeing him tomorrow."

"The son?"

"No. Gregory."

"I know it is unjust, Father Dowling, but even despite the way things have turned out, I cannot like the man. After all, he left the priesthood."

Now, in that same study, Phil was saying, "Cy wanted Jacuzzi to bring some kind of charges against that son of Barrett's. If Quirk hadn't made the same demand, maybe Cy would have. I wouldn't blame him."

"Well, the son's plan certainly worked. So what is Agnes Lamb's theory?"

"Remember this is all speculation. Wild speculation."

"But Agnes Lamb is a good officer."

"The best. Her attention has turned to the other son, Madeline Murphy's undoubted son. A kid named Marvin."

Agnes Lamb had returned to the Murphy house after the excitement of Tetzel's story and its subsequent retraction. Given the way Marvin lived, she was fairly sure he would be at home, and so he was, once more on the back patio, wearing jeans and a sweatshirt and open-toed sandals. He seemed to be growing a beard.

"Do you read the papers?" she asked, pulling up an aluminum chair.

"Just the *Wall Street Journal* and *Financial Times*."

Agnes expressed the surprise she felt.

"I'm into investments," Marvin explained. "Do you realize the number of people who make money off other people's work? What is stock but a lottery ticket taken on the performance of a company? You bet, others bet, the price of the stock rises, and then you pull out with your winnings and begin over again. It could give usury a good name."

"You're against capitalism?"

"I'm all for it. I won't tell you how much I've made in the past week alone. And I do it all on the computer, where you can get a broker who doesn't charge an arm and a leg. That's what I'd like to be, eventually, a broker. He bets on the betters, only he can't lose. He's like the owner of the casino."

"I meant the local papers."

"Their financial news is more than a day old when they print it."

"I wondered if you had read the story about the DNA tests."

Marvin grinned slyly. "Mom told me. That's why you wanted to know about my toothbrush, isn't it?"

"Well, I wasn't checking on dental hygiene."

"What a stunt. Of course, he couldn't get away with it, but that was the idea, wasn't it? Make a farce of the whole business. I'd like to meet him." Marvin was spanking his leg with a rolled-up *Wall Street Journal.* "You know what I was imagining? We were brothers."

"That's the way it looked."

"Half brothers."

"You took it all a lot more calmly than he did."

"How do you mean?"

"He went about it an odd way, but he was trying to save his father's name. Why didn't you feel that way about your mother?"

"Maybe I do."

"Talk's cheap."

"Look, her main problem was Gloria Daley and Bunting. All these years and she never remembered any of that stuff until Gloria put the idea in her head. Bunting was even worse. At least Gloria accepted my mother's decision to let it drop, but he was going to write about it anyway. Well, he won't write about it now."

"His death solved a problem."

"Not the one Pasquali had. Imagine them fighting over Gloria."

"You think that's the explanation."

"Of what?"

"Bunting's death."

"My explanation? You're an officer of the law. Who brought charges against Pasquali, for crying out loud? I don't care if he goes free or not, now that Bunting's no longer around to harass my mother."

"Do you sit around here like this every day?"

"I'm an investor." He gave her a boyish smile. "I'm working even when I'm sitting in the sun. Somewhere out in virtual space my investments are rising or falling, usually rising. If they fall, I get out."

"How do you get around? Got a car?"

"It's in the garage."

"What is it, a Rolls-Royce?"

"Ha. It's one of the original Beetles. And I mean Volkswagen."

"Come on."

"It's got hundreds of thousands of miles on it and still runs like a watch. Well, maybe like a washing machine."

"Can I see it?"

"I thought you were working."

"My retirement fund is working for me. Stocks rise and fall, but I never sell. Over the long run . . ."

"Sure, sure. Put a hundred dollars in the bank when you're twelve and forget it, and when you're old you'll be rich on compound interest."

He had swung his legs off the table and got up. Agnes followed him to the garage.

"I'll back it out. You can't see much in there," he said.

He lifted the garage door and got into the car. There was a terrible racket as it started, and then it settled down and began to roll out of the garage. Once it had been blue; now it was just faded and dented, with a lot of rust. He left it running when he got out and stood looking at it with admiration.

"Not much of a trunk," she commented.

"Oh, it's not in back. That's where the motor is." He went to the front of the car, reached under the hood, and lifted it, producing an unoiled squeaking noise that went through Agnes like a knife.

"Come on, take a look," he invited.

"It's still not much of a trunk."

"Not big enough to fit Ned Bunting into?"

Later, when she told Cy about it, she described the look in his eyes when he said that: cold, distant, menacing, despite the smile.

"Was the trunk big enough?"

"I doubt it."

"He's just playing games."

"I don't think Marvin plays games." And she quoted Marvin on how convenient it was for his mother, and for him, too, that Ned Bunting could not publish his story about Madeline.

"Why does that matter?" Cy asked.

"What do you mean?"

"The story came out in Tetzel's big scoop."

"And then was shot down."

When Gregory Barrett came to the rectory again as arranged, Marie was somewhat less arctic in her manner. He was dressed in jeans, a cable-knit sweater over a checkered shirt, and loafers with a high shine.

"My working clothes. No classes today," he said to Roger Dowling in the study.

"How many classes do you teach?"

"Just two, six hours a week, Monday, Wednesday, and Friday."

"But there is also your program."

"Once a week."

Gregory looked contrite. "Compared to your schedule, I know that must seem ludicrous."

"But you have to prepare for classes, read papers, meet with students. Isn't that all part of it?"

"It is."

"And you have to write your program as well as broadcast it. I should think that your labors compare pretty well with anyone's."

"The great danger of being with young people is that you begin to think you're one of them. Tommy ridicules this outfit."

"The jeans?"

"Denim. Do you know the origin of that? *De Nimes.* That's where the cloth was first made. Just a little trivia. Teaching and broadcasting makes such things cling to my mind."

They seemed to be avoiding what Greg had come to talk about. Finally, Roger Dowling asked him how it had gone with his son when they discussed the ruse he had concocted.

"I'm afraid he was pretty proud of himself," Greg said.

"Well, in any case it was discovered to be a joke."

"Some joke. Not discovered soon enough to prevent that journalist from making a fool of himself."

"Tetzel? He's had years of practice."

"Roger, the events of the past weeks have made me wonder if I know the first thing about people. You talked with Madeline Murphy?"

"I did."

"Am I wrong to think that that had something to do with her withdrawing the charges?"

"Oh, I wouldn't go that far. I told her what I told you. Paternity can be established, so it was no longer her word against yours."

"And she changed her word."

"Post hoc ergo propter hoc?"

Gregory smiled with delight. "I suppose we could sit here and trade such phrases by the hour."

"Nemo dat quod non got. That was Equivocal's variation, wasn't it?"

"What was the *mater studiorum* again?"

"Repetitio. We'd better not get started."

"I do miss all that, Roger. Not that it has a lot to do with the priesthood as such, but those years of study marked me."

"That was the idea."

"Nancy and I used to talk about the past, at first. But since Tommy came along . . ."

"I suppose it would sound odd to him."

"My father the priest."

Roger Dowling said nothing. When Gregory spoke again, he avoided Roger's eyes. "I think you know what was the worst thing about what Tommy did."

Again Roger Dowling waited. Gregory did look at him now, and there was anguish in his eyes. "He thought I was guilty, Roger."

"Did he say that?"

"He didn't have to. What he did, and the reason he gave for it, said it all. First proof positive, then the revelation of the hoax, and I'm off the hook."

"Well, you're not exactly without resources, Greg. Why not have a real test run on you and Marvin Murphy?"

"What would be the point of that?"

"I'm just an old celibate and don't understand these things— father, son—but if I had a son who thought I was guilty of such a charge, I think I would want to answer in kind."

Gregory's initial negative reaction gave way almost to excitement at the prospect. "Do you think the boy would agree?"

"Why wouldn't he? I think you both ought to go to a lab and have them take what they need and settle it once and for all."

"But it is settled."

"I meant for your son."

"How would I find out if Marvin Murphy would be willing?"

"I'll look into it, if you like."

* * *

He talked to Agnes Lamb about it, and she wanted to come along. "This is one weird fella, Father. I want to hear his reaction to the idea."

Marvin was at his computer, buying and selling, and asked them to go out onto the patio while he finished up. Outside again, Roger lit his pipe, and Agnes leafed through the book on the metal table. "It's all about people who made a zillion in the market."

"Lives of the saints."

Agnes looked puzzled. He did not explain. Don't we all need models of what we are trying to become?

"I don't suppose you ever played the market, Father," Marvin said, when he came out and threw himself into a chair.

"No."

"I wish my mother were here. She was really impressed by you."

"It was mutual."

"You mean that?"

"Of course. She exhibited great courage at a very difficult time in her life. You know that there were those who proposed that she just get rid of you."

"She might find it more attractive now."

"I've come to ask a quite particular question. You know how Thomas Barrett set up a hoax of a DNA test."

"Officer Lamb has told me all about it."

"How about a genuine test?"

"Genuine?"

"You and Gregory Barrett go to a lab. I don't know what it is they need for a good test. A little blood? They run the test and then we all know—"

"Father, my mother has dropped the whole idea. It really wasn't her idea anyway. She's not a strong woman. I mean, she's very susceptible. She got talked into it, and now she's sorry, and that's that."

"What Thomas Barrett did is being taken to suggest that all these charges are fantastic."

"This one was."

"But the test wasn't a test." He busied himself with his pipe. "It would be a way of making it up to Gregory Barrett."

"Making what up?"

"His good name has been subjected to a great deal of abuse. Why do you suppose his son did what he did?"

"So what did happen would happen."

Roger shook his head. "He thought his father was guilty."

Marvin thought about that. He wore corduroy slippers with no socks, and his jogging outfit looked as if he had slept in it. His hair was as it had been when he got out of bed. Portrait of a capitalist.

"And you want proof positive that he's innocent?"

"Why not?"

"It would just be one more game. You plan to ask Tetzel along?"

"Will you do it?"

He shook his head. "Did you ever listen to Barrett's program on NPR?"

"Have you?"

"What a know-it-all. He talks about books and authors as if he owned them."

"Or as if he admired them."

Again Marvin shook his head. "That isn't the way he comes through to me. I had teachers like him. Real pains in the shall we say neck. No, he's come out of all this smelling like a rose. How about my mother?"

It was what Roger had hoped he would say.

"She wouldn't like it?"

"I wouldn't like it! The worst part of this whole business is that her name is mud and there isn't any test that can change that. You say she was courageous. Okay, she was. She is. Her life has not been a walk in the park. That zoo of a branch library she works in! She went into library science because she loves books, and she ends up babysitting a bunch of perverts. Gloria Daley kept after her when she learned about me. Who the hell is my father, anyway? There were photographs of a sailor she said was my father, but it turns out she bought the damned pictures at a yard sale. I could wring Gloria Daley's neck. As for Ned Bunting . . ." His voice had risen but now subsided. "Speak well of the dead, right?"

Tuttle brooded. He could not believe that he had been such a bad judge of Thomas Barrett. Oh, he had been fooled in his day. More often than not, if the truth were known. Look at the way Hazel had established herself in his office. She had come in as a temporary. Maybe a day or two, he had told her, just to clean up the files, put things in order, a few letters. A day or two! Before the first day was out she had taken on a permanent look. Of course, she was nice to him then, very deferential—Mr. Tuttle this and Mr. Tuttle that—and she had been as remote as a nun. It had been the line of least resistance to let the arrangement go on. She was an efficient, docile woman who would be at his beck and call. Once she was established, once he owed her more than he would have wanted to pay in a lump sum, she began to emerge from her disguise.

"I'll put it on the tab," she said, and her smile had altered. "You can pay me later."

She had already severed relations with the temporary service that had sent her. She and Tuttle seemed to have entered into a pact. Then she got personal. "Doesn't Mrs. Tuttle ever come to the office?"

"My mother is dead."

"I meant your wife."

"Me? Married?" The very thought of it struck terror in his breast. For one thing, girls had always laughed off any advances on his part. For another, he had the model of his parents' marriage, back there on the South Side, two devoted and contented spouses whose love for their son created a warm cocoon against the world.

"Divorced?"

Tuttle frowned. His parents' marriage had become the standard for him. Till death do us part. He never took divorce cases, and he told Hazel that. "You make at least one enemy. Usually two."

She sighed in a way that lifted her enormous breasts. How mammalian she was. "You're telling me?"

He did not want to know about her personal life. She made it clear to him that she did not intend to remain single. "That's why I'm a temporary. No long-term career commitments. I've seen too much of it."

He had been impressed by her résumé. For half a dozen years she had been a legal secretary in a prestigious firm in the Loop.

"How many partners are there?" he asked. What a comedown for her to be working for a freelance attorney who had to scrounge for a living.

"Dozens. And more hands than partners, if you know what I mean."

Tuttle didn't know what she meant. She explained. He blushed.

"I knew right off that you're a gentleman."

By degrees she became the tyrant of his office. The first casualty was Peanuts Pianone, the one true friend Tuttle had, even though the officer was all but autistic. They got along. They had often sent out for Chinese food and pigged out in Tuttle's office. Peanuts was Tuttle's conduit to what was going on at police headquarters, suggesting what ambulance he might chase. It was Peanuts who had told him of Agnes Lamb's theory, overheard when she was talking to Cy Horvath. Of course, Peanuts thought it was crazy.

"Either he goes or I do," Hazel said when she was cleaning up after one of their impromptu lunches. Styrofoam boxes, balled-up napkins, beer cans, bottles, a mess. This ultimatum might have been Tuttle's last chance at freedom. How could he not prefer Peanuts to Hazel?

"Get rid of her," Peanuts advised. It might have been another ultimatum.

Ah, how he would recall with sighs those happy bachelor

days. Hazel made him feel like a married man. No wonder he was determined to remain single. Now Peanuts came no more to the offices of Tuttle & Tuttle. It softened the blow to think of it as Peanuts's decision as much as Hazel's.

So he had been wrong about Hazel. She had led him up the garden path. Thomas Barrett was different, though: a clean-cut youth, top of his class, on the wrestling team, admitted to Notre Dame, though that came after the boy had come to Tuttle. It was Thomas's concern for his father that touched Tuttle's heart. Here was an emotion he understood, one of the purest known to man. Thomas wanted to exonerate his father. He had collected materials so that a DNA test could be made. He entrusted them to Tuttle, and the rest was history.

It had been a trick. Thomas had provided materials from his father and from himself, and of course they matched—but that was taken to mean that Gregory Barrett was the father of Madeline Murphy's son. The accusation had been withdrawn, but now tests had proved it true. Tetzel took the ball and ran with it, only to find that he was heading for the wrong goalposts. So Tuttle brooded.

The one catch in the whole scenario was young Barrett's claim that it was Marvin's toothbrush. Tuttle had not asked him how he had managed to get it. He gave Thomas a call. "Tuttle here. Where can we talk?"

The direct approach always put the other person at a disadvantage. But Thomas laughed and said, "So you can give me hell for misleading you?"

"Oh, that's ancient history now. This is something else." He had crossed his pudgy fingers.

"You could come to the house, I suppose."

And run the risk of having to confront father and son together? "Do you know a restaurant called the Great Wall?"

"Never heard of it."

"I'll tell you how to get there."

Thomas took the instructions and repeated them as if he were writing them down, but Tuttle was not confident he would come. Not that it would be a complete loss. He could have lunch anyway.

They were to meet at one o'clock. The hour came and went; Tuttle ordered. Then Thomas arrived. Tuttle waved his chopsticks, then his red paper napkin, and Thomas came to his booth.

"I thought I'd get started," Tuttle said.

"You're going to eat all that?" Thomas was genuinely surprised.

"Didn't you ever eat Chinese?"

"That sounds like cannibalism."

"Oh, the meat is some kind of rodent."

"Let me just have a little of the rice."

Tuttle pushed the bowl of rice across the table. "There are chopsticks there."

"I'll need a fork." Thomas unzipped his jacket and tried to tuck a napkin into his turtleneck. His hair seemed damp. "Fresh from a shower. I run on Wednesdays."

"No classes?"

"Reduced classes. I'm a senior." Also, Tuttle had learned, the class valedictorian.

Thomas finished the bowl of rice and looked speculatively at the other dishes. Tuttle gave him samples from several, and soon those were gone.

"You ought to order now," Tuttle suggested.

Thomas shook his head. "That will hold me. So why are we meeting?"

"So I could assure you I'm not as dumb as I am. I didn't even ask you how you got hold of a toothbrush of Marvin Murphy's."

"I would have lied."

He was quick, Tuttle had to give him that. "Did you ever meet him?"

"Why would I?"

The reasons Tuttle thought of might seem romantic. A hitherto unknown half brother?

"Father Dowling has come up with an ingenious idea."

This information was one of the bonuses of knowing Peanuts. Peanuts dismissed the idea, since Agnes was involved, but Tuttle liked it.

"You staged a fake test; let's have a real test."

"The test was real enough. The results were misinterpreted. My DNA matches my father's. Big surprise."

"By real, I mean testing Marvin and your father."

"To prove they aren't related?"

"Exactly."

"We already know that."

"No. We know that you and your father are related."

Thomas sat back in the booth, his shoulders pressed against it. A big kid, 175, maybe 180 pounds, and no fat—but he was a runner, and a wrestler.

"You're making this up, aren't you?" He tried to get an answering smile from Tuttle. "I don't believe anyone seriously proposed such a test."

"Marvin's against it, too."

Thomas seemed surprised, but he thought about it. "That makes sense. Who needs more bad publicity?"

"Did you ever meet him?"

Thomas looked at Tuttle. "Did he say we met?"

"I haven't asked him."

"I'll save you the trouble. We haven't."

Agnes had told Cy about the old VW Bug in the Murphy garage. He was not exactly encouraging her fantastic theory that Marvin might have done away with Ned Bunting. The problem was, they had nothing else, not even another fantastic theory. Pasquali had been released, thanks to Marie Murkin's certainty that she had seen him in St. Hilary's Church during the time period in which Bunting met his death. At least the head librarian of the Benjamin Harrison branch had had a motive. He was a rival for the affections of Gloria Daley, and he had flipped Bunting on his ear to prove it. It would have made more sense if Bunting had done in Pasquali. Tuttle had acted as if he regularly got charges against his clients dropped.

"Good try, Horvath, but it was a waste of taxpayers' money," the lawyer said in parting.

"I was going to ask you about that."

Tuttle, his hat at a jaunty tilt, had started off with Pasquali, but now he turned. "Ask me what?"

"Oh, I'll let the feds explain it to you. I told them I knew nothing about your finances."

Tuttle's triumphant smile dissolved into doubt and worry. A small victory, but when one has been bested by such a one as Tuttle, small victories count. It didn't make up for the way Tuttle had made a fool of him with those envelopes of evidence.

"How were you to know?" Pippen asked. They were having coffee in the courthouse cafeteria, where Cy had come after sending a confused Tuttle on his way with Pasquali.

"I got them from Tuttle." She waited. "Tuttle. You know Tuttle. I just took his word for it."

"No, you took the word of Gregory Barrett's son. At second hand."

When Cy had told his wife about the phony test and where the materials had come from, she laughed. That was about what it deserved, but it was nice to have Pippen sympathetic.

Pippen was a problem for Cy Horvath. He loved his wife, and even if he didn't he wouldn't cheat on her. The world was going to hell in a handbasket, and he was not about to speed it on its way. Even so, in some remote world of the imagination, he wondered what it would have been like to meet Pippen when they were both free to do something about it. Pointless speculation, as wild as Agnes Lamb's theory about Marvin. Cy had a wife and Pippen had a husband. Nonetheless, on the job, they were buddies. *She probably thinks of me as a big brother,* Cy told himself. *A dumb big brother.* The trouble was, he didn't think of her as a sister. Her willowy body, her mischievous green eyes, her thick golden hair gathered into a ponytail or, sometimes, a long braid that bounced off her back—these added up to beauty for Cy.

Still, he prided himself on the conviction that she had no idea in the world what his real feelings for her were. Feelings, not thoughts, not plans. He had talked about it in the confessional with Father Dowling.

"Impure desires?" the priest had asked.

"No, nothing like that."

"And no acts?"

"Never."

"So why are you confessing it?"

"I feel badly about it."

"Maybe you should try to see less of the woman."

"All right."

"Innocent as it has apparently been, she seems to represent a possible occasion of sin for you."

"Oh, no, Father, I would never do that."

"As Adam said to Eve."

Cy agreed to see less of the woman, nameless there in the dark. The whole process was anonymous and intimate. Roger Dowling was the same man behind the screen as he always was, but in the confessional the priest wasn't Father Dowling and he wasn't Cy Horvath. Even if Roger Dowling had suspected who the penitent was, he would have erased the thought. That made the confessional the only place Cy could talk about his odd attraction to Pippen.

He tried to see her less often, but the more he tried, the more he ran into her. So his not wholly unwelcome problem continued.

Now, in the cafeteria, he told her about Agnes Lamb's suspicion of Marvin.

"I suppose that makes sense," Pippen said.

"I'd like to know how. The harm has been done to his mother. She had retracted her charge against Gregory Barrett. So Ned Bunting threatened to write it up anyway. Barrett's kid has made a mockery of DNA testing. The smart thing to do would be to let it fade away."

"But is he smart?"

"He's kept an old VW Bug running."

"The original?"

"This might be one Hitler drove, according to Agnes."

"I don't like the new ones."

"It's pretty hard to find an old one."

"I'd like to see it."

Cy realized that he wanted to see that old car, too. Pippen went back to the cool of the morgue, and he signed out a car and just drove. He was as accessible in his car as in his office, and there wasn't much going on. These were arguments that he really wasn't wasting his time.

When he turned into the street on which the Murphys lived, the old VW was just starting away from the curb, making quite a racket. Cy passed it, glancing at Marvin behind the wheel, made a U-turn, and followed.

Smoke poured from the exhaust of the little car, and Cy thought of pulling him over. Just a thought. Marvin lurched along, doing a lot of shifting, laying a lot of smoke. Then he arrived at his destination. The Benjamin Harrison branch of the public library. He put his car in a handicapped spot and loped toward the door. Cy called in for a tow truck.

The crew could have lifted the little VW onto the flatbed, but they put down the ramps and used their towing apparatus, being careful how they hooked on. They didn't want to get the front bumper and leave the car. Cy sped them on their way, not to impoundment but to the lab.

He figured going along with Agnes was no dumber than going along with Tuttle on the DNA test. The lab people could check out the car and see what they might see.

"Beware of answered prayers," Gloria said to Pasquali. They were in her studio, among dozens of finished and unfinished canvases. "What if I had been a successful painter?"

Pasquali looked around. "Some of these look pretty good."

"As good as those you hung in the library?"

"People talk about them." He seemed to be choosing his words.

Gloria had been charmed by the thought of Fred saying a novena so that all would go right with them. If only he had some fire in him. Ned had wanted to be a writer—in the worst way, as Gloria had come to think, and his wishes had been fulfilled. Not even Gloria could find much to praise in the piece he had written about Father Dowling. Now, when she remembered Fred laying Ned Bunting out on her front lawn, she almost resented this treatment of the former usher. Then again, Fred had acted because of her. The two men had been fighting over her, hadn't they?

"How long before you retire, Fred?"

"Retire? I'm nowhere near sixty."

"You can do what you do anywhere, can't you?"

"What do you mean?"

"Haven't you ever wanted to just get away from Fox River? Go somewhere interesting. Taos, Santa Fe . . ."

"Is that what you'd like to do?"

"No one's asked me."

Men are so manipulable. He pulled his chair closer to the stool on which she sat, wearing a smock, her easel before her. She let him take her hand.

"Let's talk about it, Gloria."

Well, that was more than Ned Bunting had wanted to do. Oh, he would talk, but he'd had his own idea of paradise.

"San Miguel de Allende. I read about it in a writers' magazine. The cost of living is low, wine is cheap. I could write in the daytime, you could paint, and at night . . ." His voice had grown husky.

"Where is it?"

"Mexico."

"Mexico! Not on your life."

Fred was saying that he would look into library jobs in New Mexico when her cell phone rang. She plucked it from her pocket.

It was Maddie, all excited. "Someone has stolen Marvin's car! He parked it in front of the library, and when he went out it was gone. Then he just disappeared."

"Have you called the police?"

"He was looking for Fred Pasquali."

Gloria smiled at Fred. "Has he gone over there?"

A pause on the line. "Isn't he with you?"

"Did you suggest that to him?"

"Tell Mr. Pasquali the vagrants are back at the computers."

The line went dead.

"Maddie," Gloria reported.

Fred looked guilty. He was playing hooky. Ever since his arrest, he had been an infrequent presence in his office at the library.

"Marvin's car was stolen and he's run off somewhere, and she thinks he's lost."

"Madeline is a very jumpy woman."

Gloria patted his hand and stood. "Coffee?"

He came with her into the kitchen. While she made the coffee, Gloria considered how unjust it was that Maddie had turned on her. If anything, recent events should have brought them closer together. Of course, Maddie had listened to Marvin when he told her that none of this would have happened if she hadn't listened to Gloria. Alas, there was truth in that, Even so, Gloria had no regrets. When Tuttle had turned up those records of how Gregory Barrett had counseled Maddie, a picture began to emerge for her. Women had to stand together.

They were still waiting for the coffee to finish when Marvin banged on the door. He came in furious, as if Gloria were responsible for the theft of his car, but Pasquali was his real target. "What kind of a library are you running down there? My poor mother has to spend her day tolerating vagrants at all the computers. A person can't even park his car there without it being stolen."

"There's never been a car stolen from the parking lot of the Benjamin Harrison branch," Pasquali said, answering anger with anger.

"Parking lot? I parked it in the street."

"In the street?"

"In front of the entrance."

"But there are no parking places there, unless you're handicapped."

"What difference does that make?"

"If I were you, young man," Pasquali said, calm now, "I would call the police garage and see if my car hasn't been impounded."

"I wasn't there more than . . ." Marvin wasn't sure how long he had been in the library after parking on the street. His mother, when he found her, was distraught because the vagrants were once more at the computers. Marvin solved that problem immediately: He went to the bank of computers and unplugged them all.

A snarling chorus went up as the monitors went blank. The men jostled together, and one became their spokesman. "Why in hell did you do that?"

"Time out for some technical troubleshooting, gentlemen. We should have these back in service in a week or two. Meanwhile, I suggest you take your business to the Theodore Roosevelt branch. Any policeman can give you directions."

And he led his mother away. "They'll plug them in again," she said.

"I doubt it. I'll unplug them. Better, I'll deactivate the electricity in that area. Where is the fuse box?"

Pasquali's office. Unlikely, but they went in there.

"Mom, you've got to get out of this place."

"Where would I go?"

"Florida?"

"Florida! My vacation isn't for months."

"I don't mean a vacation. Look, I've made some money lately, quite a bit of money. We can afford the move. If you want to work in Florida, okay; if not, well, that's okay, too."

"You'll take care of me?"

He hugged her. "Turnabout is fair play."

She ran her fingers over his bearded face as if she were trying to find there the lineaments of his father's.

"They want me to take a DNA test with Barrett."

She stepped back. "That's nonsense."

"Of course it is, but it will clear the board. Then we drive off to Florida and put it all behind us."

"In your Volkswagen?" But she was hugging him again.

When Pasquali said that Marvin's car had probably been ticketed and towed, in the phrase, a light dawned in the young man's eyes. "Gloria, can I borrow your car?"

"What for?"

"Just for an hour or so."

Gloria looked at Fred. He lifted his shoulders. Doubtless he wanted to get the young man out of the house. Gloria got her car keys and gave them to Marvin.

"Do you have my cell phone number?"

They exchanged numbers, and then Marvin was at the door.

"I like your beard," Gloria said.

Sometimes Roger Dowling thought that his study in the St. Hilary's rectory was a kind of clearinghouse, leaving him with more information than any of his informants. Marvin, it turned out, had agreed to the test. Maybe he wanted proof positive of who he wasn't. Who said it is difficult to prove a negative? Amos Cadbury.

"I just hope it is kept confidential," Amos said.

"I don't think either one would want it otherwise."

"And Gregory Barrett will be definitively exonerated?"

Roger Dowling nodded. Gregory's motive in agreeing to the DNA test with Marvin had become clear to him. Gregory didn't need the proof, but his wife and son did. What Thomas had done, as Gregory had said, indicated that Thomas thought him guilty. And Nancy had gone along with it.

From Phil he had heard of Tuttle's doings in the wake of his disillusionment with Thomas Barrett. "He wanted to tell him he should have asked how he had gotten hold of a toothbrush that was allegedly Marvin's. Do you know what he answered? 'I would have lied.'"

"Where did they meet?"

"The Great Wall. I don't know why Tuttle has an office; he does most of his business in that restaurant. Thomas came in fresh from a shower."

"It was raining?"

"No, no. It was his regular jogging day, and he took a shower before going to the Great Wall."

"What day was that?"

Phil thought. "Wednesday."

"Still no leads on Bunting's death?"

Phil groaned. "We actually impounded Marvin's car and had the lab people look it over. Nothing." Marvin had been a wild idea of Agnes Lamb's, but Phil did not criticize her. After the release of Pasquali, they had to try something.

"What next?"

"We thought about Gloria Daley. She came up with a theory about Pasquali killing Bunting, throwing him into the river, and then driving her up there to discover the body. So we thought maybe that's what she did." Phil looked at Roger Dowling. "But she didn't. After we impounded Marvin's car, he borrowed Gloria's and came down to make a protest. He knew his car hadn't been taken away simply for parking in a handicapped space. That's when he demanded that we examine Gloria's car as we had his."

"And you did?"

"Clean as a whistle."

"Somebody killed Ned Bunting."

"When you figure out who, let me know. I'll listen to the wildest theories."

* * *

When the theory came, Roger called Cy Horvath. If the huge Hungarian lieutenant was surprised by his suggestion, he gave no sign of it—but then his face seldom revealed what he thought. "I'll look into it."

It was the remark that Wednesday was Thomas Barrett's usual day to jog that set Father Dowling's mind going. Ned Bunting had been killed on a Wednesday. The following Wednesday, Cy was waiting when Thomas emerged from the Barrett house in shorts and a sleeveless T-shirt and a blue and gold headband. Before he went out of sight, Cy emerged from his car wearing a sweat suit and a pair of tennis shoes endorsed by Michael Jordan. He was not in the shape he had once been in, but he thought he could run as far as Thomas Barrett.

Thomas took the road that led across the bridge to the west bank of the Fox River, moving easily along, while Cy became aware of his heavy breathing, and of the fat that seemed to have gathered around his middle and bounced as he ran. Once he had been a star athlete who could run the hundred in record time all suited up for the game, but that had been a long time ago. Cy began to think longingly of the car he had left a block from the Barrett residence. As the distance from it increased, he was more and more conscious that it would be the same distance back.

The boy ahead seemed tireless as he ran along the path beside the river. If only he would take a rest, but that seemed out of the question. They were approaching the parking lot called lovers' lane, and suddenly this pursuit seemed to make sense. When Cy got to the parking lot, there was no sign of Thomas, and he headed for a bench and collapsed on it. He looked north up the river road but could not see young Barrett. He had learned though, that the scenario Father Dowling had sketched was not impossible. Then someone sat beside him on the bench.

It was Thomas, and he seemed hardly to have worked up a sweat. "Are you following me?"

"Why would I be doing that?" Cy was panting, and sweat ran down his face.

Thomas handed him a towel. "You're out of shape."

"I haven't done this for a long time."

"Wednesday is my long run."

"Is this your usual route?"

"Why else would you be following me?"

"Do you know who I am?"

"Not your name. But you're a cop, aren't you?"

"That's right."

"This is where Ned Bunting's body was found."

"On a Wednesday."

They sat in silence for a while. Then Cy said, "Tell me about it."

"Oh, I won't make it that easy for you."

"All I ask is that we walk back to my car."

"What for?"

"People are more willing to talk when taken downtown."

"So let's talk."

Cy told him what had been gathered at the crime scene. Footprints galore, those of Pasquali and Gloria Daley, of course.

"Even when we eliminated those of the examining crew, there were several unidentified sets." He pointed at Tommy's feet. "What size are your running shoes?"

"Eleven."

"That's about right. You shouldn't have left the bat."

"What bat?"

"A Louisville Slugger. It looks like a collector's item."

Tommy was staring at him. "Who told you about that?"

"It's yours, isn't it?"

"I have a bat like that at home. How did you know?"

"Why don't you show it to me?"

The way back was no longer than the way they had come; it only seemed longer. A silent Tommy Barrett walked beside Cy. There wasn't much to say. Either Cy's stab in the dark would be disproved or . . . But his legs were so heavy, thinking was a chore. He settled down to just getting back to the Barrett home.

The house was empty. Tommy let them in and led the way to a rec room in the basement. He stopped halfway across the room, then turned. "It was my bat you found."

"Is this a confession?"

"I thought people were more willing to talk when you take them downtown."

Cy looked at the kid. "Your bat is missing?"

He nodded. Cy would have given anything if there had been another Louisville Slugger in the Barrett rec room.

"You want to change first?"

"What's the point?"

So they went out to Cy's car, and on the drive Tommy talked nonstop. Ned Bunting had to be stopped. He was destroying his father, destroying their home. Even his mother had begun to wonder about the charges against her husband.

"So you took care of the problem?"

"I'm willing to answer for what I did."

9

The new twist in the events that had dominated so many minds for weeks brought gloom to everyone involved.

Tuttle tried to find something noble in what the boy had done. "He did it for his father."

If so, he had sacrificed Ned Bunting as well as himself. Phil took no satisfaction in the solution of the crime, but there was no room for doubt. The bat was Tommy's, and his running shoes matched prints taken from the scene of the crime—and he was a willing witness against himself until Amos Cadbury assigned young Tim Fuller from his firm to represent the boy and he was made to keep silent.

"Fuller will make sure he has the best defense possible," Amos said, but his tone seemed to rule out any possible verdict of innocence.

Marvin tried to see Tommy, but his request was refused, even when he suggested he was a relative. He wasn't; the second DNA test had proved a negative definitively: Marvin was not the son of Gregory Barrett. Tetzel wrote a skeptical piece on the dangerous reliance on laboratory tests to establish guilt or innocence—sour grapes, of course.

It was Madeline Murphy's reaction that was surprising. She came to the rectory and wept when she told Father Dowling that she felt as she would have if Marvin had done such a thing in order to defend her good name. When Marie brought in tea for the caller and found her weeping, she took the woman in her arms and they cried a duet.

"Mr. Pasquali has resigned," Madeline said, when she regained control of herself and sat sipping tea. "They are moving to New Mexico."

"They?"

"He and Gloria Daley."

"Gloria Daley!" Marie cried. "None of this would have happened but for her."

"I don't blame her," Madeline said. "I was a fool."

"Now, now," Marie said.

"I have turned in my resignation, too, Father. Marvin is taking me to Florida."

"Marvin?"

"He seems to have the Midas touch with the stock market."

If Madeline's visit had been emotional, it was far worse when Gregory and Nancy Barrett came. There was no weeping, no emotional outburst, simply the stunned reaction of two people who felt they had been smitten by the hand of God.

"Now, Greg, you know that isn't true."

"If I hadn't left the priesthood, if I hadn't married—"

Nancy bristled at this. "Greg, for heaven's sake."

Father Dowling told them of Madeline Murphy's analogy. Marvin might have done such a deed for her.

"That woman," Nancy said. "I told you once I hated her. I'll say it again. I hate her."

Father Dowling, remembering Cy Horvath's account of Tommy's confession, remembered the boy's motivation when he had concocted the phony DNA test. "He tried to protect you once before, Greg."

"Dear God."

"I can't believe they will find him guilty," Nancy said. "Anyone could have thrown that bat there."

"True. And anyone could have worn a pair of your son's running shoes and made the prints found there."

Greg just looked at him. How could he take comfort in such a fantasy as that? Nancy looked away, an angry expression on her face.

Father Dowling said, "There is only one way to save him."

"How?" Greg asked, his voice strangled.

"If the person who killed Ned Bunting confesses."

The silence that followed this remark grew deeper.

"Nancy?"

"What?"

"Surely you don't intend to let your own son answer for what you did."

Gregory leapt to his feet, his face distorted with anger. "Roger, I can't believe you said that."

Nancy remained seated. Slowly she lifted her face to her husband's. "I never thought that they would trace that old bat to Tommy."

"What are you saying?"

"If you think Tommy could have done this for you, don't you think I would have?"

"Nancy . . ."

But she was nodding. "I called that man and asked him to meet me there. I parked up the road when I saw he was seated on a bench. I crept up behind him with the bat." She breathed deeply and closed her eyes. "It was horrible. I couldn't just leave him there. I tried to lift him and I couldn't. And then I saw that sheet of plastic lying in the woods—"

"For God's sake, Nancy, stop it. None of that happened."

Her eyes were full of tears. "I would give anything if it hadn't. But Greg, Father Dowling is right. I can't let Tommy suffer any more. These past days, oh my God . . ."

It was half an hour later that Roger called first Amos Cadbury and then Phil Keegan. Meanwhile, he and Nancy had spent ten minutes alone in the front parlor. Mercy had been received. Now justice would make its demands.

In a sad bid to redeem his lost credibility, Tetzel spent several hours with Henry Drummond, listening to the accountant's charges against the archdiocese. If the two of them hadn't been drinking, it would have been time utterly wasted.

"This Barrett thing makes them look innocent as lambs,"

Drummond mourned. "They were down for the count, and look at them now. No one is interested in their real crimes." Drummond meant the fact that he had been fired. The problem was that the accountant was the only one who charged himself with financial peculation. The archdiocese had smothered the whole episode in ambiguous prose. No mention at all of wrongdoing on Drummond's part. "Oh, the cunning, the clerical cunning of it all."

"Let's have another drink," Tetzel suggested.

"What do I have to drink to?"

"How about three in the morning?"

Drummond thought about it. "I'm game."

At the end of August, Tommy Barrett went off to begin his first semester at Notre Dame. His father drove him down. It was not the joyful occasion it might have been, but things could be worse. Fuller was pleading Nancy Barrett temporarily insane, driven to the dreadful deed by Ned Bunting's harassment.

Amos Cadbury lifted his eyes when he told Father Dowling of the plea. "What would Dante have made of our world, Father Dowling?"

"Do you know the episode of Manfred in the *Purgatorio*?"

"Tell me."

A terrible man—a murderer, a tyrant, whatever his redeeming qualities—had at the moment of death cried one tear of repentance and was saved.

"How can you repent if you deny having done a thing?" Amos asked.

"If you mean Mrs. Barrett, you're wrong."

"Innocent by reason of insanity?"

"Oh, that's just courtroom jabber."

Amos thought about it. Doubtless there were things Father Dowling knew about the woman that he did not. Still, it was difficult for a lawyer to negate the demands of justice. Difficult but not impossible.

"The poor woman," he said.

"Amen."